The Soho Ripper.

A Tale from Gaia.

By Joseph Willoughby-Rainsford

Joseph Willoughby-Rainsford

www.jwrmythic.com
Twitter: @jwrmythic
Facebook: @ChroniclesofGaia
Instagram: JoeytheBard

The Soho Ripper

Written for the one who stole my heart and who is
yet to return it.

Joseph Willoughby-Rainsford

Also, special mention to;

Samir, Kieran, Ade, Alex, Lauren, Georgina and Jade who had to put up with me as I wrote this.

Another mention to my darling Jiselle who I forced to proof read my work.

The Soho Ripper

Introduction.

The story of Dorian Winters, which you are about to read, takes place almost parallel to Adrian Prince's own tale in The Mercury Key. The start of Dorian's tale begins some weeks before Adrian is delivered the mysterious key, but from there unfolds alone a similar time frame.

Joseph Willoughby-Rainsford

Part One. A Second Chance…

The rain was thundering against the concrete in a downpour the people of London knew well. It was one of many rainstorms to hit the city during the start of Autumn in September.

Most people pulled out their pop-up umbrellas, few people in Britain went anywhere without one regardless of the time of year. One person, though, did not. It wasn't because he didn't have one, or that he liked the rain, as some strange people do. No, he did not open his umbrella because at present the rain was the least of his concerns.

This was for very good reason, though, as this particular young man had just been stabbed and left, as it were, for dead.

At the moment, the knife pierced his stomach, Dorian regretted asking himself, 'How could my day get any worse?' five minutes before.

His day had begun on the wrong side of the bed. Actually, it was the wrong side of the wrong bed. Sleeping next to the *'pull'* from the night before Dorian had fallen asleep by an open window and caught a chill from the Autumn night.

Creeping out of bed, Dorian fussed over his appearance in a bathroom mirror for some time before finally being satisfied that he was as well turned out as he could be. Leaving the London flat, without saying goodbye to the person he had slept with the evening before. Dorian's nose was red and runny. It was not like him to have one night stands. Dorian was a relationship kind of guy. Or at least he had been before his last breakup a month before. Considering he'd had four different sexual partners in as many weeks, one of them being his roommate, he doubted he could continue to pretend to be innocent.

Having not been home since the morning before, Dorian was still in the same clothes. A fact his colleagues in the dingy office he worked in, noticed. The jokes he could handle but then the abuse he got down the phone from customers all day began to get to him.

Finishing his shift, Dorian found it was considerably colder than the day before. His hoodie was not really enough to keep him warm. He hurried to the tube station on Holloway Road. It was Rush-Hour, and for some reason, the Tube was even more busy than usual. Squeezing in the narrow carriage like a human sardine, Dorian travelled south on the Piccadilly line.

Getting off at Convent Garden with a glut of tourists, Dorian took in a deep breath of stale air and glared at the crowd ahead of him. Then he made his way to the lifts, only to find they were out of order.

Joseph Willoughby-Rainsford

'Sorry for any inconvenience caused, my arse.' He muttered under his breath.

Climbing the one-hundred and ninety-three steps up to the surface, Dorian had to pause for breath a few times. He really needed to stop smoking, give up the takeaways and re-join the gym.

Dorian came out of the Victorian station on St James Street. He had considered having a quick look around the shops but then decided to turn left, away from Covent Garden to avoid the milling crowds of tourists and sightseers.

Then he headed towards Soho, cutting through Seven Dials. He had been lucky enough to get a three-bedroom flat in the thriving Gay and Music centre of London. On his own, he would never have been able to afford it on a Call Centre salary. However, sharing with two friends, they were able to afford it, just about.

Taking shortcuts through the alleys, like he did every night, Dorian began to relax as it started to drizzle. He was going home to watch TV and order Pizza while stalking his ex-boyfriend online.

'Oi, you give us your phone and wallet.' Said a man as he suddenly appeared out of the shadows. Dorian tensed as an icy shiver of fear crept into him. He couldn't believe it. A mugging. He was being mugged.

The Soho Ripper

About to tell the man to 'Fuck Off', Dorian stopped himself as he felt the presence of three others behind him. Like an antelope on the African Savanna, Dorian knew the eyes of predators were on him.

Standing in the middle of a crossroad of back alleys, Dorian was surrounded on all sides. He must have passed one of the muggers on the way in. How could he have not noticed? Stepping backwards, as the figure in front of him loomed forward, Dorian felt a rough hand push him forward. By reflex, Dorian moved his shoulder and tried to slip between his would-be muggers. He saw a flash of silver and then felt the knife slice into him.

At first, the feeling had been strangely warm and pleasant. The heat of Dorian's blood flowed around his cold middle. It was sticky but also enjoyable, at least until the shock of pain ripped its way through his stomach.

As the knife had been withdrawn, Dorian saw the fear in the eyes of his attacker. Pulling out his phone, Dorian was about to dial nine nine nine, but the phone was snatched from his hand. Then another hand pulled his wallet from his back pocket.

As the group of muggers ran off, one of them pushed Dorian over. He fell flat on his face in a puddle. It suddenly began to pour down with rain as Dorian lay there holding his hand against his side.

Dorian didn't know too much about the human body, but he imagined the blade had sliced into one of his kidneys.

Looking up Dorian saw a distant crowd on a busy street. He tried to call out but found his voice was quiet and weak. There was no way he could be loud enough to be heard. As Dorian looked down, he noticed the puddle he was leaning in was completely red. How much blood had he lost?

Dorian then heard a footstep and looked up again. His vision was beginning to blur, but Dorian saw the silhouette of a slender young man standing above him and looking down. He couldn't be sure, but Dorian thought the man bore a sinister grin.

'Hello, Dorian. Your day has taken a turn for the worst, hasn't it?' Said the silhouette. Reaching out a hand, Dorian hoped this person had come to save him.

'I am afraid there's no hope for you now. You have lost too much blood. No ambulance would make it in time. Your life is over, or I should say your human life is. Fear not, though.' The silhouette produced a small phial and held it up. The glass caught the light from a window and glowed red in the man's hand.

'Who are you?' Dorian whispered quickly.

'Me, I am an outsider to these parts. A bemused traveller and purveyor of second chances. My full name is ancient and hard to pronounce in your language. Some have called me the Master of Deals; others know me as the Stranger, but you my dear Dorian, you can call me May-Hem.' May-Hem spoke with the voice of a young but well-spoken teenager, like one of the Chelsea boys Dorian saw from time to time.

'Help me!' Dorian pleaded, confused with why this person was taking so long to call for help.

'I have in my hand a small sample of blood. Don't let its size fool you, though; it is more than enough to save your life. If you want it, then we need to form a contract.' A long piece of tattered paper appeared in May-Hem's hand from nowhere. 'I understand you are not in the best position to sign at the moment, so let's say if you chose to drink the contents of this phial you agree to the terms of the agreement. Of course, you are wondering what the terms are, well I am not sure you have enough time for me to go through them all. The important detail is, from time to time I shall call on you to work for me, and of course, I shall take one thing from each of your trophies, but I will collect this myself. Do you agree.'

May-Hem crouched over Dorian and offered him the phial in a gloved hand. Up close Dorian could see the young man's handsome face, with high cheekbones, a Roman nose and eyes of pure darkness. Anyone seeing this young man, dressed in his white trainers, jeans and black hoodie, with the hood up over his slightly long hair, they'd have thought him a typical teenager. Until you saw his eyes, you wouldn't notice anything special about him. The eyes were dark pits.

Feeling life slipping away from him Dorian grabbed the phial. He pulled out the cork and then pressed the glass to his lips. The red contents quickly entered his mouth. It was salty and metallic like a one pence coin.

'Oh, one more thing,' May-Hem began, 'I shall leave you with my mark, so you don't forget me.'

May-Hem clicked his fingers, and suddenly Dorian felt a burning pain on his chest. Then the burning pain was blocked out by the suddenness of an extreme agony which flared its way through his whole body igniting every nerve ending within him.

Dorian let out a scream of pain and then knew only darkness.

The Soho Ripper

Part Two. Family Butchers.

Dorian awoke in his bed with a thundering headache.

Had it all been a dream? Cautiously, Dorian reached a hand down and pressed it against his side. The skin was smooth and hairless, with no sign of breakage, bruising or scabs.

Letting out a sigh of relief, Dorian lay back down and grazed his hand slowly up his body. Then he felt something crusted and rough on his chest. Bounding out of bed, Dorian ran naked to the mirror and looked at himself.

To his surprise, he appeared to be a lot skinnier. His love handles were gone. His stomach was flat. Not only that, he had a six-pack. Not a true one formed over years of training but one from being so skinny his small muscles pressed out against his tight sickly pale skin. Dorian had always been pale, but now it looked as if his body had never seen the sun. He looked like human veal.

The most alarming change, though, was on his chest. On his left pectoral, directly over his heart was a mark. It looked like a recently healed brand mark as if someone had taken a white-hot iron brand and pressed it against his skin. The mark was strange too, some glyph similar to those he saw in graffiti on the side of churches. Touching it gingerly, Dorian was surprised when he felt no pain. Perhaps last night hadn't been a horrible dream.

'You alright?' Asked a familiar voice.

Turning around, Dorian saw his roommate Phil standing in the doorway to his room. Phil was in a pair of boxers and a grey t-shirt, which didn't completely cover his hairy ex-jock belly.

Used to having his roommate walking in and out of his room whenever he wanted, and having slept with him a few times, Dorian didn't mind the fact he was naked. He did mind the mark on his chest though, so he quickly grabbed his bathrobe and pulled it around himself.

'You look ill.' Phil said with a raised eyebrow. 'Are you feeling alright?'

'I'm starving.' Dorian said honestly. He would worry about the mark and last night later; now he had a need to feed.

'Well, Leroy is making his health smoothie now if you want some.' Phil said with a snare.

'No, I'd rather eat my own sick.' Dorian joked.

'Can I borrow your laptop?' Phil asked, heading over to Dorian's desk already.

'Of course.' Dorian replied.

Following Phil out of his bedroom, Dorian saw his other roommate Leroy standing in the kitchen. Leroy was the tallest of the three of them and the only straight guy in the household. His girlfriend

The Soho Ripper

Lauren was dressed in her morning jogging outfit and doing stretches. She had the body of an Olympian, and although Dorian had no interest in women, he could see why Leroy was head over heels for her.

'See you later, babe.' Lauren said, giving Leroy a kiss on his stubbled cheek. 'Later boys.' She called to Phil and Dorian as she left.

'Later.' They both waved.

'What you making today, Leroy?' Phil asked.

'Banana, blackberries, blueberries, raspberries, strawberries, apple juice and honey. You want one?' Leroy asked in his thick French accent.

Like his girlfriend of two years, Leroy was athletic. Thick muscles rippled under his tight t-shirt and hoody.

'God no.' Phil chuckled.

'How about you, Dorian?'

'No thanks, Leroy. Is there any leftovers, though?' Dorian asked hopefully.

'There is some of my steak left in the fridge if you want it. Lauren and I are going out tonight, so I will be, how do you say, hungry.' Leroy grinned to himself.

'Thanks.' Dorian said. 'I'll shower, then have it.'

'I'll be in my room, job hunting.' Phil said, closing the door.

Joseph Willoughby-Rainsford

'I'm going to work in a minute, so have a good day Dorian.' Leroy said, dropping the last slice of banana into the blender.

When Dorian returned to the kitchen, damp and clean, he walked straight to the fridge. There was an intense hunger building up inside him. Hunger so extreme like he had never felt before. Dorian grabbed the plate the two steaks were on. They were both cooked but still blue in the preferred French style. Being a proud Brit, Dorian pot a frying pan on the cooker, covered it with oil and began to fry the steak until it was well-done all the way through.

At first, the steak had smelt so good. In a way, Dorian had never noticed before. However, by the time he had finished cooking it the scent had soured. Dorian put the well-done meat on a new plate. Cutting a thick slice and seeing it brown all the way through, Dorian popped the meat into his mouth and began to chew.

A second later Dorian spat the meat out. It tasted rancid. Rushing over to the sink, Dorian put his lips to the tap and began to drink. The water was ice cold but cleared away the horrid taste of the meat. Had those steaks gone off? Dorian looked at them. They looked fine. The still bloody one looked beautiful and smelt delicious.

Not wanting to risk it, Dorian was about to put the uncooked steak in the bin, when he caught the scent of it again. Before he knew what, he was doing, Dorian grabbed the steak with his hand and took a huge bite. With some primal urge, Dorian did not chew the meat but began to suck it. The red juices flowed into his mouth and tasted astonishing.

When he had finished, Dorian pulled the steak out his mouth and was surprised by the change. It reminded him of the orange ice lollies he had as a kid. He would always suck the end of them drawing out the flavour and leaving the clear ice behind. It seemed like he had done the same to his steak. The red blood was gone, and all that was left was the dead grey meat. Dropping the meat into the bin and throwing away the one he had cooked, Dorian went back to the fridge. There were no steaks left.

Still starving, Dorian washed his hands and then got dressed. He didn't start work until the afternoon as he was on the evening shifts this week. He decided he could go to a Butchers and get some more prime steak.

Although it was cloudy, Dorian still found it too bright. He pulled out his designer sunglasses and zipped up his jacket to his chin. Now suddenly slimmer, Dorian's clothes felt baggy. The wind seemed to get within them and tickle his skin, but he didn't feel cold. Now that he thought about it, he didn't feel warm either. He didn't seem to feel temperature at all.

Dorian wondered if he should be worried about that, but right now the only thing on his mind was getting rid of his hunger. It was as if his body was eating away at itself. As if there was something alive in his stomach wanting to be satisfied.

Holding his stomach, Dorian walked into *"Johnson's and Son's Family Butchers"*, the store Leroy got all his meat from. As soon as he entered, Dorian heard a tinkle of the bell above his head, but it sounded like he was standing under Big Ben. The noise made him jump. The old man in a blue and white striped apron looked surprised as Dorian glared at the small bell.

'Can I 'elp you, young man?' Asked the Butcher. 'You not fully up yet.' Dorian guessed this was Johnson.

'Loud bell you've got there.' Dorian said.

'Eh, hung over, are we.' Commented Johnson. 'You will be wanting some bacon and eggs then, just the thing for a hangover.'

'No, no.' Dorian said, guessing he probably did look like he was recovering from a night in the town. 'I was looking for...'

Dorian's nose caught the scent of something delicious. He looked to his left to see a man in a farmer's cap, jacket and big woollen scarf. The man looked eager as another Butcher behind the counter handed him a sealed bucket.

The Soho Ripper

'Here you are, Mr Morris, five litres of pork blood as you requested.' Said the other Butcher.

'Thank you very much,' the old man said as he handed over a few notes, 'my family loves it when I make black pudding.'

'You still there, lad?' Asked Johnson.

Dorian's eyes looked back at Johnson, and he heard himself ask, 'How much for a litre of pig's blood?'

Leaving the shop and its confused owner with his new purchase. Dorian hurried back to his flat. The smell of the container in his hand was driving him wild. He couldn't wait. He ran to the nearest alley and found a quiet spot between two industrial bins behind a Chinese restaurant.

Opening the tub, Dorian threw away the lid and put the rim to his mouth. With a small part of himself feeling disgusted, Dorian drained the tub in seconds and then dropped it to the floor. As the white container bounced and rolled away, Dorian leant against the brick wall and felt his stomach. Never before had anything felt so good.

It was like the time when Dorian had smoked weed at university, but a thousand times better. Licking his lips, Dorian closed his eyes and gently rubbed his flat stomach.

He was there for some minutes until he heard a nearby door opening. Not wanting to be seen,

Dorian quickly hurried away. As he ran down the alley, he felt full of energy and life. He felt incredible. He wanted to run, so he did, going faster and faster.

The Soho Ripper

Part Three. A Soft Touch…

As the midday sun remained hidden behind the thick dark clouds over central London, Dorian ran down the alleys of Soho.

He was so alive and so ecstatic. Never before had his body responded so well to him. He wondered if this was how Leroy felt all the time. Maybe this was why he had his meat so bloody, but then Leroy didn't drink tubs of pig's blood.

The realisation of what was coursing through his system caused Dorian to stop in his tracks. He was at a crossroad of alleys. The Crossroad in fact where he'd been stabbed. Looking down, Dorian saw the puddle of his own blood. Memories of last night came flooding back. He pictured the face of his attacker and remembered the scents of the others. A few yards away was his brown leather wallet, now empty of cash but his cards, none of them contactless, were still there. There was no sign of his phone though.

Rage began to fill Dorian, and there was a burning sensation on his chest. Unzipping his jacket and unbuttoning his shirt, Dorian peered down at the ugly red mark. It was glowing like the end of an incense stick.

'They say criminals always return to the scene of the crime,' said a voice Dorian thought had come from a nightmare, 'but few realise it is the victims who are drawn to the spots where their lives are torn apart.'

Turning around Dorian saw May-Hem, still in his hoody and jeans and sitting on a window ledge.

'You are the one who saved me?' Dorian asked, trying to see the young man's shadowy face. The figure nodded. 'Did you get me home too?' The figure shook his head. 'What do you want?'

'What do I want?' The figure jumped down from the window ledge and smiled warmly at Dorian. 'Now that's a question for the ages. I guess as an Earth-born human, you know nothing of...my kind. I must admit I am new to these parts and find your ways both strange and enchanting.'

'Earth-born human?' Dorian asked. 'You some nutter who thinks he is an alien?'

'It is not nice to insult the person who saved your life.'

'It's not nice to brand people either.' Dorian pointed to his mark. 'What did you do to me?'

'The mark is in the terms and conditions of our contract. Working in the corporate market, as you do, you know the importance of branding. It's so others may see the products I have on selection.'

'Who are you, really?'

'I told you. My dear fellow, you can call me May-Hem.'

'That's not really a name though...?'

The Soho Ripper

'And where I come from the name Dorian is odd. It takes all sorts to make worlds.'

'You said you wanted me to do things for you. What kind of things?'

'It was all covered in the contract.' May-Hem yawned.

'But I didn't get to read it.' Dorian snapped.

'You should never sign a contract before reading it.' May-Hem waved a finger.

'There was no time.'

'There is always time for the important things. Anyway,' May-Hem spoke louder to stop Dorian from interrupting, 'I have no jobs for you at present, so you keep enjoying your new-found strength and abilities. When I need you, you will know?'

May-Hem turned to walk away, but Dorian reached out for him and was about to shout, 'Wait.'

May-Hem turned his head and glared at Dorian with eyes filled with hate. Feeling sudden fear, Dorian lurched back. Then May-Hem's pleasant expression returned, and he stood there in silence.

'Erm, what did you do to me?' Dorian asked after a few seconds of silence.

'Now that is almost the right question.' May-Hem gave Dorian a boyish grin. 'I however, did not do anything to you. I simply gave you a phial, which you under your own free will drank. The contents of said phial are what has changed you.

You are a glorious thing, the first of your kind in this world.'

'First what?' Dorian choked.

May-Hem walked past Dorian and said. 'That, my dear Dorian, would be telling.'

When Dorian turned around, May-Hem was gone.

As Dorian got back to his flat, he found Phil laying on the sofa and watching trashy daytime television. The slightly older man was still in his boxers and t-shirt. His face had a two-day stubble, and a thick unwashed smell clung to him. Stronger then Dorian thought it should be.

'You need a shower, mate?' Dorian said, almost angrily.

For the last two weeks, Phil had been home every day. He had lost his most recent job for smoking weed in the toilets and now was job hunting again. In the few years they had lived together, Phil had gone through eight different jobs to Dorian's one.

Dorian worked in a Call Centre for a Corporate Business and Private Clients Accounting Firm. Leroy was self-employed as a personal trainer. Phil on the other hand, worked temp jobs and bar jobs and some office jobs, never one job for long. Even so, he still had the most money as his rich family gave him a monthly allowance. Dorian guessed it was to keep him away from home. Phil lifted his arm and at once the smell intensified.

Taking in a big sniff, Phil fake coughed and said. 'Yep, you are right.'

Getting up, Phil walked to the bathroom, leaving the empty pizza box and drinks can on the coffee table.

Dorian hated mess so he quickly went to tidying up. By the time, he had cleaned the debris of Phil's unproductive day away, the chubby ex-jock was out of the shower and standing naked in the kitchen.

'Ahhh, you cleaned up after me. Thanks mate, you're the best.' Phil beamed, going to the fridge and grabbing another cola can. 'You look much better by the way; the air must have done you good. The colours back in your cheeks.'

Dorian ventured into his room and glanced at his reflection. The mirror must have had a layer of condensation on it as his reflection was blurred. Dorian was about to clean it off when Phil walked naked into the room and jumped on the bed.

'What are you doing?' Dorian asked.

'Wanna bang?' Phil gave Dorian a hopeful look.

'No.'

'Oh, come on, it's been ages since we last had fun.'

Dorian shook his head.

'But you really enjoyed it last time.' Phil pleaded.

'No means no, Phil.' Dorian felt angry.

'Fine. Suit yourself.' Phil said testily before strolling out of the room.

As soon as he had left, Dorian went about making his bed. He tidied his room while he was at it and then heard a shout.

Rushing back into the kitchen, Dorian saw Phil holding his finger and wincing in pain.

'What happened?' Dorian asked.

'I cut my finger on the fucking knife.' Phil cursed.

'I'll get the first aid kit.' Dorian quickly went to the cupboard.

As he approached Phil, his nose caught a delicious smell. It was similar to the pig's blood but better. So much better. Like the scent of freshly baked bread compared to pre-sliced loafs. Before he knew what, he was doing, Dorian had taken Phil's bloody finger and put it in his mouth. Phil looked puzzled for a second and then grinned.

'I thought no meant no.' Phil said as he gently moved the finger in and out of Dorian's mouth.

Dorian did not reply as he sucked on the finger and tasted the blood. It was the most delicious thing he had ever tasted. Much better than any cocktail or champagne. Richer than any wine. Sweeter than any juice. More intoxicating than vodka.

'Ouch!' Phil said suddenly, pulling his finger away. 'You bit me.'

The Soho Ripper

With the finger gone, Dorian felt as if he had just woken up from a dream. 'Did I?' He glanced down at Phil's finger. 'Sorry, I got too into it, I guess.'

'You are strange, and your teeth are so sharp.' Phil complained, and he sucked his own finger.

Feeling his hands begin to shake, Dorian stepped away from Phil. 'I'm going to go to work mate.' He said, hurrying away.

Joseph Willoughby-Rainsford

Part Four. Club Milkshake.

With another draining and mind numbing evening shift out of the way, Dorian left his office with a feeling of unease.

What was happening to him? During his lunch break, he had tried to eat a ham sandwich and a packet of crisps, but the bread tasted stale, the ham mouldy, the butter rancid and the crisps felt like dust in his mouth. Looking at each of the items after gagging, he saw none of them were off.

Now the sensation of hunger had returned. He remembered the taste of Phil on his tongue and felt his jeans get tighter. Dorian checked his reflection in a shop window, but it was too murky to see. Must have been the poor lighting, he guessed.

It was just a quarter past eleven at night. The clubs in Soho would now be at their peak. People would be feeling properly buzzed with the music and alcohol pulsing through their veins. Dorian imagined being on the dance floor in the middle of the mass of bodies, he'd be surrounded by men all hungry for each other. He'd find one; he'd take them to a back alley and then he'd drain them dry.

No! Where had that thought come from? It was something primal and profound. The urge had been there. Similar to the urge for sex or food but it was both of them, and it was much stronger.

The Soho Ripper

Blinking, Dorian found himself on the tube. He didn't even remember getting on it. He must have changed at Holborn because he was now on the Central Line approaching Tottenham Court Road.

As the tube stopped, Dorian pushed his way off against the wall of bodies. The busy people of London paid him no notice as they continued on their journeys.

After a few minutes of heavy breathing, Dorian righted himself and then fussed with his hair. Without looking, he knew every hair would be perfectly in place. Suddenly he was no longer worried, but knew what he was going to do. He would head back to the flat, shower, change, and go clubbing. The night was calling to him.

When he got back to the flat, he found both Leroy and Phil sitting on the sofa and watching some sort of sport's game. Dorian nodded to them and quickly headed into the bathroom. In less than ten minutes he was in his bedroom, dry and standing naked looking out of his window at the Soho street below.

On his bed behind him, Dorian had laid out a pair of black jeans, a skinny fit black shirt and his black leather jacket. Dorian didn't know why but he felt like tonight would be a good night to wear all black.

Once dressed, Dorian strolled confidently out of the flat, without a word. Both Leroy and Phil were too busy chanting at the television to notice him.

Outside the air was fresh and crisp. Dorian breathed in deeply and walked purposely towards the nearest club. It was one of the newer ones, below a restaurant. The only entrance was a staircase down into a cellar, guarded by a pair of big bald bouncers.

'Evening gentlemen.' Dorian said as he approached them.

'You are looking sharp tonight.' Said the younger of the two bouncers. Dorian knew he had seen him before but did not recall his name. 'Where's your friend...Phil?'

'Oh, he's watching some men kick a ball about a field.' Dorian sighed. 'So, I decided to go out hunting.'

'Hunting?' The other bouncer looked at him curiously.

'Just my little joke, are you going to let me in, boys.' Dorian gave them his best winning smile.

'Go on then.' The younger bouncer winked at him.

'Thank you, gentlemen.' Dorian kissed them both on the cheeks and then walked down the steps.

Inside the club, the air was close and filled with the mixed scents of manly musk, fruity cocktails and the ever-dense fog of weed. Dorian took in a big whiff and wandered straight onto the dance floor. Club Milkshake was a novel experience. Bright and colourful the interior looked like a candy shop with giant jars of sweets forming the pillars. The bar offered all the usual cocktails you would expect but also a large selection dairy confections from ice cream sundaes with rudely shaped bananas to alcoholic milkshakes.

Club Milkshake was having an Eighties night, with the music blurring out so loud the voices of all were consumed. The bar was crowded with people trying to get deals from the all night Happy Hour. Dorian felt thirsty but fancy cocktails and foaming shakes were the last thing on this mind.

As he danced, he made eye contact with a few different men. Most of them he glanced over as they were not to his taste. Then he saw a beautiful blonde, blue eycd boy. At a guess, Dorian would have said the boy was twenty or at the least nineteen. He was clean shaven, shy looking but wore the latest trends and had the newest haircut, short sides with curls on the top.

Still dancing, Dorian slowly made his way over to the boy who looked happy and slightly alarmed to be approached by him.

'Hello, I am Dorian.' Dorian said, putting an arm around him and looking into his eyes.

Joseph Willoughby-Rainsford

Part of Dorian was surprised at how confident he was acting. Usually, it would take a few shots of vodka before he was able to go up to someone and start a conversation.

'I'm Ben.' Said the youth with a nervous smile.

'What are you drinking Ben?'

'A Cosmo. Do you want one?'

'No, I never drink...alcohol.' Dorian heard himself saying.

'Are you a health freak?' Ben asked.

Dorian chuckled. 'You could say that. Now, Ben, I am going to kiss you.'

Ben just nodded, and Dorian put one hand on the back of the youth's head. Bringing him in close, Dorian pressed his lips against Ben's and could taste the sickly-sweet Cosmopolitan.

With hunger welling up inside him Dorian pushed his tongue into Ben's mouth and tasted him. He had to stop himself from biting the boy's tongue and so pulled away leaving Ben looking dazed.

'Don't stop.' Ben cooed.

'Let's get out of here.' Dorian heard himself say.

Less than two minutes later, Dorian was walking down an alleyway around the corner of the club with his arm around Ben. Stopping out of sight of the main street, Ben leant back against the brick wall and looked up into Dorian's eyes.

The Soho Ripper

Leaning down and in, Dorian pushed Ben's head to one side and gently nipped at his ear and then began kissing his neck.

'Oh, that's so good.' Ben whispered as his hands began to caress Dorian's crotch.

Dorian ignored the attention of the young man as he tasted the sweet, salty skin on his neck. He knew the shower gel the young man used, the shaving cream and the after shave. He could tell from the senses on his tongue all the ingredients used to make the products the boy had used like a sommelier knew what was in wine with their nose.

Then the hunger gripped his stomach again. It was stronger and more urgent than before. It was a need for a fix. It was primal. It was instinctive. Dorian felt his teeth changing shape, and in alarm, he pulled away.

Ben leant against the wall in a daze. There were dark red love bites across his neck but no rips or breakages.

'Don't stop. Please.' Ben begged.

Shaking his head, Dorian stepped back again. His teeth felt large and sharp. He felt the desire to open his mouth and snap like a viper onto the neck of the youth.

With all the will he had, Dorian turned and ran as fast as he could away from Ben. The young man called after him, but Dorian did not look back.

Joseph Willoughby-Rainsford

When he was a few streets away, Dorian checked his pockets for his phone. He could call Phil and Leroy and get them to come and get him. After patting his pockets in vain for some time, Dorian remembered with a pang of anger that it was stolen when he had been stabbed. His mind felt fuzzy and confused every time he tried to concentrate on those fateful moments.

Letting out his anger, Dorian punch a nearby wall. To his surprise, his fist went directly through the old brickwork. Warily pulling his hand out, Dorian expected to see bruised and bloody knuckles, but his hand was undamaged.

Then Dorian heard a scream. It was a woman's scream and not one of someone messing around or seeing a rat but a scream of real terror. Dorian didn't hesitate a second; he ran towards the scream. His ears had been able to pinpoint the woman's location. She was in the next alley to him. Within seconds he was there.

It took Dorian less than half a second to fully examine the scene in front of him. Between two industrial bins a lady in her mid-twenties, wearing a skirt and leather jacket was being pressed against the wall by a man, she was both frightened of and disgusted by. This man was rough looking and held a knife to her neck. His trousers and boxers were around his ankles, so his spotty white arse was on show as he thrust at the woman.

The Soho Ripper

In two strides, Dorian was at the side of the man. Then grabbing the man, he turned him around and pushed. The man cursed as he was pulled away from his victim. Then as Dorian unleashed his full strength, the man flew backwards and smashed into a wall with a cold crack, before landing in a heap of rubbish bags.

The woman now free shivered and collapsed to the ground. She brought in her knees as she looked up at Dorian with a tear and mascara stained face.

'It's alright.' Dorian said reaching out a hand.

'Thank you.' The woman sobbed as Dorian pulled her to her feet.

'Come on, let's get you out of the cold and I will stay with you as you call the police.' Dorian said, putting a comforting arm around the woman. 'I'm Dorian.'

'I'm Jade.' Said Jade, leaning against Dorian. 'Thank you so much.'

As Jade leant in Dorian could smell her perfume but also a stronger and sweeter smell her blood. Glancing down Dorian saw the cut on her neck. The man must have scratched her with his knife as Dorian pulled him away.

They were still in the alley, a few yards away from the street and completely in shadow. Dorian felt an overwhelming thirst. He needed to drink. He needed to feed. Feeling his mouth and teeth changing shape again, Dorian was taken over by instinct.

He suddenly pushed Jade against the wall and was on her. One hand held her head to her side, and the other pressed her hand against the wall. In surprise, Jade let out a shriek, but it was cut off when Dorian's jaws clamped around her thin neck. Feeling his teeth rip into the soft pink flesh, Dorian began to drink the blood. He was in ecstasy.

Dorian drank and drank as Jade struggled against his growing strength. Never before had anything felt so astonishing as it entered his system. Dorian did not see the woman he held as a person; she was a glass of his favourite drink, and he intended to drain every last drop.

As Dorian continued to drink pint after pint of Jade's blood, the woman started to fight back. She began to punch Dorian in the head with her free hand and then frantically began to scratch her face. Ignoring her at first, Dorian felt his hands twitch as Jade began to stamp on his feet.

Without pulling away from her neck, Dorian brought up his right hand to Jade's stomach, but it wasn't a hand anymore. His fingers had lengthened, and his nails had sharpened to talons. As he drew his hand across Jade's stomach, his claws sliced her tender skin and stomach muscles to ribbons.

Jade started to scream and using the last of her strength pushed Dorian away. As a part of Dorian realised the horrible things he was doing he loosened his grip and allowed himself to be pushed away. At the same time, the primal side of him fought back, a taloned hand slashed across Jade's neck. The claws sliced her throat to the bone and Jade died in an instant.

Her bloody and shredded corpse fell to the ground as Dorian stared in horror at what he had done.

Joseph Willoughby-Rainsford

Part Five. Blood Angels.

Dorian lay in his bed in a red haze.

It had been two days since he'd killed Jade and in that time, he'd not left his room. Laying naked on his covers, Dorian stared at the cracks in his ceiling as he tried to concentrate. He was still in a daze with a warm red haze flowing through his system. Jade's taste was still on his tongue. Her blood was still in his veins. Surprisingly he could see her memories in his mind's eye as if he was watching a lifetime's worth of home movies.

Through this strange connection, Dorian learned of Jade's happy childhood in a small Hertfordshire town. Dorian could see how Jade had gone travelling around the world after she'd finished her course in Leisure and Tourism. Dorian found out Jade held a special place in her heart for New Zealand. Seeing the memories flash within his mind, Dorian knew what it had felt like to stand on top of the mountains and see the untouched land spread out until it reached the sea.

As the memories continued to dance through Dorian's mind, the young man found out Jade had come home after heartbreak and moved in with her sister. Those memories were more painful, and so Dorian did what he could to block them out.
Both Leroy and Phil had knocked on his door a few times, but he had told them he had the flu and

refused to unlock the door. Using the house phone, while his roommates were out, Dorian had called his office and told his manager he had the flue as well. From his laptop, he had seen the reports on the news.

"Gruesome Murder in Soho."

"Woman Slashed and Man Bludgeoned."

"Frightful Murder Leaves London in Shock."

Not only had Dorian killed Jade, but he had also killed her rapist. Jade's attacker turned out to be a middle-aged manager called Jamie Halt with a wife and four children. At the time, Dorian had only wanted to save the woman, he had not realised his strength would have thrown Jamie so far and so hard, nor had he thought it had killed him.

As he laid there, Dorian had wanted to cry, but no tears came. He couldn't sleep either and no matter how long he was awake for he was not the least bit tired. Part of him now began to realise what he had become but he couldn't believe it. They... Those things were not real... The creations of the medieval mind only made real in Hollywood blockbusters and hit TV shows.

As much as he knew that to be true, Dorian could not deny the blood he had drunk and the memories now swarming in his mind. Nor could he deny his strength, speed and increased sense. He was becoming sensitive to sunlight too and worryingly his reflection was fading. Now even in a clean mirror, he was a blur like an ink-smudged newspaper.

As much as the guilt ate away at him, a growing part of Dorian really wanted to experience it again. The sense of pleasure and power he felt when drinking was...there was no other way to put it....it was better than sex.

So, Dorian remained in his bed, his door locked as he continued to watch Jade's life unfold within his mind. It was now three in the morning according to his alarm clock. Getting out of bed, Dorian walked to the window and opened it. He breathed in the cold city air and took in the scents of a hundred-different people. It was almost as if he could see smells now.

The whiffs of scents drifted through the air like coloured smoke leading to their source. Dorian took in a big breath and was amazed by the amount of information he got. He knew his neighbours were doing weed and two men down the street had eaten a curry that didn't agree with them. One person smelt of fear as he tried to work up the courage to ask for a girl's number.

Then Dorian's nose got a scent he recognised. The scent filled him with rage and hatred. Grabbing a pair of jogging bottoms, Dorian slipped them on. He then headed to his door but heard someone walking to the fridge. From the sound of the heavy steps, Dorian knew it was Phil getting a midnight snack.

The primal side of Dorian took over again. Dorian turned, ran and then leapt out of the window. Wearing only his joggers, Dorian landed in the empty street as gracefully as a cat jumping off a fence. Getting up, Dorian turned and ran towards the scent. All four of them were there. Less than a mile away. Dorian had them.

A few minutes later Dorian was in an alleyway, looking up at an open window of an abandoned office building. The signs around the building said it was soon to be demolished.
Dorian guessed his attackers were using it as a base of operation in the meantime. On impulse, Dorian jumped and on hitting the wall of the office building he started to climb. His hands and bare feet were able to find purchase on the solid wall, and he quickly made his way up to the window.

From his hearing alone, Dorian could tell there were only four men in the room beyond. None near the window. From scent, he could tell all four where the muggers who had left him for dead.

Peeking over the window ledge, Dorian saw the four men gather around a table. They were smoking, drinking and chatting to each other. All were relaxed and seemed proud of themselves. Dorian saw mattresses and sheets against one wall, and on an old desk was a pile of belongings. From iPods, Smart Watches, Jewellery, Handbags and as his eyes focused Dorian saw his own phone.

Before his eyes, Dorian saw his hand's change. Once again, his fingers lengthened, and his nails sharpened and turned to thick, razor sharp claws. Then Dorian pulled himself through the window and quietly stood behind the four men.

'Good evening, gentlemen.' Dorian said in a calm and controlled voice.

The four jumped up in fright and looked at Dorian in astonishment. They fumbled with their knives in their drunken state.

'Bleeding 'ell!' Shouted one of them.

'Where the fuck did you come from?' Said another.

'It's just a boy; he's not even dressed.' Pointed out the third.

'I know you!' The fourth glared at Dorian.

'I am sure you do.' Dorian said, as he felt his face changing shape and heard his voice deepening.

Under his skin, Dorian felt his cheek bones spread out and rise. His ears twitched as they lengthened into points. His jaw changed shape as a top and bottom set of fangs grew between his teeth.

'What the fuck are you?' Trembled the first man.

'I am the stuff of nightmares.' A voice from within said using Dorian's mouth.

The Soho Ripper

Dorian opened his eyes.

He was laying in blood. The corpses of his four new victims were spread out around him. It was now sunrise, and so Dorian had closed the blinds to stop the sunlight creeping in.

He had slashed apart the legs of the four men to stop them escaping and then sliced out their tongues to stop them calling for help. Then he had drained them one by one. Now he lay in the blood he had let escape, moving his arms and legs to make a blood angel.

With what mental strength he had, Dorian found he could push out the memories which seemed to come with the blood. So, he never learnt the names or life stories of his muggers, nor did he want to. With his new-found ability, he pushed out Jade as well, freeing his mind from her and freeing himself from guilt.

'Well done, Dorian.' Said an all too familiar voice.

Looking up, Dorian saw May-Hem sitting on a chair with one of the newspapers from the day before. A headline about Jade's murder was on the cover.

'I think you shall make the front page again.' May-Hem grinned, dropping the paper onto the bloody floor. 'You are quickly adjusting to your new life, and now there are five fewer criminals in the world, and one less lovesick and desperate woman. Did you feel no remorse for the lives you ended?'

Dorian stood up. He felt so much stronger and looking down at his red soaked chest; he saw his muscles were bulging under his slim frame.

'You made me a vampire, didn't you?' Dorian asked.

'Yes, but not just any vampire. The blood you ingested is from Cesare Borgia.' May-Hem grinned.

'Who?' Dorian asked, crossing his arms.

'The spawn of Dracula himself.'

'Dracula is real?'

'Well not on your world, but where I am from.'

Dorian frowned, he was growing tired of these word games.

'What do you want this time?' Dorian snapped.

May-Hem smirked and clicked his fingers. The mark on Dorian's chest began to burn, and Dorian fell to his knees in pain.

'Careful, Dorian, my boy.' May-Hem said calmly. 'You don't think I would have given you such power and strength without an insurance policy.' The pain faded, and Dorian glared at May-Hem with hate. 'You have only scratched the surface of your powers.' May-Hem continued. 'I look forward to seeing you discover the rest of them. But this is not a social call; I have a job for you. On the chair, next to me I have left you some

The Soho Ripper

information about a person who broke their contract with me. Find them and kill them. Also, help yourself to everything behind you.'

May-Hem pointed at the desk covered in stolen goods. Dorian looked at it, and when he turned back, May-Hem was gone.

Grabbing a rucksack from a corner, Dorian took it to the desk and quickly went through the items. Putting them one by one into the bag Dorian found; four smart phones, five watches, six rings, two engagement rings, three tablets, one laptop, a pair of stylish leather shoes, two bracelets, an E-Reader and two-thousand-five-hundred and sixty-eight pounds and twenty-four pence in cash. Last, he picked up his own phone from the desk, it was out of battery but seemed otherwise unharmed. Then going over to the chair, Dorian took a sealed envelope, which he also put in the rucksack.

It was still sunny outside, and people were crowding the busy London streets. So, Dorian searched through the other bags. Finding a pair of jeans and a hoody not covered in blood, Dorian put them on. Then an idea struck him. He quickly grabbed the vodka bottles and poured the remaining contents on the bodies and the floor. Then taking a lighter, Dorian lit the flame and dropped it onto the nearest body. At once, the flames rose up.

Joseph Willoughby-Rainsford

Part Six. Memoirs of a Diva.

'Four more bodies were discovered in the Soho area this afternoon, following a fire in an abandoned office building on Wardour Street the day before.' A news anchor-man said during the evening news. 'Although severely burned the bodies of four men are still unidentified they seem to have similar wounds to those on Jade Moorberry also found in Soho last week.'

'Fucking hell.' Said Lauren, as she cuddled up with Leroy on the sofa.

Phil was sat next to the pair and looked equally as shocked by the news and images on the screen. 'It's only a few streets away; that's scary.'

'This is nothing, compared to the crime rate in Paris.' Leroy said, glancing at his phone.

'It's still horrible, though.' Lauren playfully hit Leroy. 'Don't you think, Dorian?'

Dorian alone was not watching the television. Standing behind them in one of his newly purchased all black outfits, Dorian was unloading his shopping bags and putting his tubs of pig's blood and juicy steaks in the fridge.

'Yes, it's downright awful.' Dorian said, feeling a slight thrill as he spoke.

'What's in those tubs, mate?' Phil asked, craning his neck round.

'Nothing for you.' Dorian replied tartly.

The Soho Ripper

'Alright, I was only asking.' Phil sighed.

'It's pork blood, no?' Leroy asked as he glanced back.

'Blood! Yuck.' Lauren and Phil said, almost in unison.

'What do you want that for?' Phil asked.

'It's an ingredient.' Dorian stated.

'Our Dorian is becoming a body builder, like his best buddy Leroy.' Leroy said with a grin. 'Pork blood is rich in riboflavin, vitamin C, protein, iron, phosphorus, calcium and niacin. Plus, it is easy for the body to digest and absorb.'

'A body builder?' Phil looked Dorian up and down.

'Can you not see his new muscles bulging under that shirt.' Leroy commented.

'The only person to get over the flu and suddenly develop a six pack.' Phil laughed. 'You're a lucky son of a bitch.'

'Leave my mother out of this.' Dorian said with a wink.

'Police are asking anyone who has information to come forward. Soho has been shaken by these recent crimes and the Metropolitan Police has said they are increasing their presence in the area.' The anchor-man continued.

'I hope the Feds catch this bastard soon!' Phil said.

Joseph Willoughby-Rainsford

'Coppers, Phil. We don't have Feds in the United Kingdom.' Dorian said as if speaking to a child.

Finished putting his shopping away, Dorian walked into his bedroom and locked the door behind him. He had taken to locking the door now to stop Phil wondering in. He feared when he was thirsty, the horny Phil might become a victim.

Alone in his room, Dorian pulled out the folded letter from his back pocket. He had read the note inside more than a dozen times, but he read it now once again.

Dorian,

The time has come for you to start paying back your debt and I have a special victim in mind for you. I am sure you have heard of the famous Opera Diva, Lady Penny Oakwood.

Well, you'd never guess, but ten years ago her voice was like a bag of cats being swung around. She made a deal with me to have the voice of an angel, and anyone who has heard her sing can tell, I clearly delivered.

Now ten years on, my deal is almost complete. She is to return the voice and offer payment, but she has refused and gotten herself some bodyguards who have ways of keeping me out her townhouse, but these wards won't work on you, my dear Dorian.

The Soho Ripper

Go to twenty-four Saint James's Place, find her in her boudoir and taste the blood of the Prima Donna.
Have fun,
May-Hem.

Just the thought of not completing this task made the mark on Dorian's chest feel warm. He never wanted to feel pain like that again. It had felt as if a white-hot pole was lancing through his chest about to singe his heart.

Putting the letter away, Dorian left his room again, wave goodbye to his friends, still engrossed in the news and prepared to leave.

'Stay safe.' Lauren called after him.

'Don't worry about me, my dear; I reckon I'm the most dangerous thing out there.' Dorian winked.

'Don't let the muscles go to your head.' Leroy called.

A week or two ago, Dorian would have gotten the tube down to Green Park, but now full of stolen life Dorian wanted to test his new body and abilities.

Using his impressive upper body strength, Dorian climbed to the roof of his building and stood tall looking out across Soho. He was glad to be heading out of Soho tonight, too many victims in the area would make things very uncomfortable for him.

With his regained phone, Dorian had tried to take a few selfies, only to find the picture showed nothing but a translucent blur. As annoying as it was, this fact at least meant he didn't have to worry about security cameras. Also, as his hands and feet and other features seemed to be changing, he wasn't worried about leaving fingerprints. He wasn't sure if toe-prints where a thing, but if they were, he was fine there too.

Now Dorian jumped from roof to roof as he travelled south over the streets of Soho towards Piccadilly and then onto the royal district beyond, near the Ritz. Travelling this way, Dorian was surprised at the speed he made it across the city. It was much faster than a tube and being above the streets he didn't need to deal with the crowds.

Having scouted out the address earlier that day, Dorian had found from Green Park he had a clear view of the Saint James's Place gardens and the backs of the stylish mix of townhouses. From the front, the doors were guarded and the windows barred, but Dorian had not seen, smelt or heard anyone towards the back of the property.

Jumping off the roof of the Ritz, Dorian strolled confidently down the path in Green Park to his target. The people who passed him didn't give him a second glance as Dorian willed himself not to be noticed. This was another ability he had recently discovered. When arriving late to work he'd hoped his manager wouldn't see him until he got to his desk. The startled surprise of his manager, when he found Dorian sat in his seat after looking right through him as he passed, made it clear this was something else Dorian could now do. Testing the ability on Phil later that day, Dorian had enjoyed standing in the room and moving things Phil was looking for every time his roommate's back was turned.

Reaching the back of the fence cutting off the garden from the park, Dorian focused on remaining unseen and then jumped. He landed in the middle of a manicured lawn cornered with four large bowl shape plant pots. Carefully Dorian walked towards the tall townhouse in front of him and when he reached the back door of the house he was surprised to find it was being opened.

Frozen, Dorian watched as a man came through the door. The man pulled a packet of cigarettes out, put one in his mouth and then lit it. Closing the door behind him, the man then looked up and looked directly through Dorian. He started to walk forward as he smoked and Dorian quickly got out of the way.

Then as the man smoked in the garden, Dorian got a good look at him. This man looked as if he had come off a film set or out of a Comic Book Convention. He was dressed in a long black leather jacket, which looked like a combination of a World

War II officers trench coat and a medieval doctor's coat. The man had long brown hair and sideburns, giving him the appearance of a Victorian gentleman. Then Dorian noticed the blue runes stitched into his clothing and daggers tucked into the man's belt. Was this man one of the guards May-Hem had mentioned?

Turning away from the man, Dorian walked to the wall and began to climb. Glancing down from time to time to make sure he had not been noticed, Dorian crawled up the side of the building like some comic-book hero.

When reaching each floor, Dorian paused and listened. He heard more guards wandering the corridors and other people chatting and moving things about. Dorian could tell somehow; his target was not on that floor and so moved on upwards. The small part of Dorian, which still listened to his moral compass found it easier to refer to Lady Oakwood as a Target instead of a person. It made what he was about to do easier to swallow.

On reaching the top floor of the townhouse, Dorian found himself near an open window where the curtains drifted lazily in the breeze. Peeking inside, Dorian saw a lavish room decorated with handcrafted items of furniture. The furniture appeared more suited to a palace then a townhouse. On the far wall was an oil painting of the Target in an ornate golden frame.

The Soho Ripper

In the middle of the room, the Target stood in a Japanese silk bathrobe, considering a full-length mirror. The mirror did not show the Target's reflection. Instead, it rippled like water as it showed the image of an older stern-faced woman in a suit.

'You requested this meeting, Lady Oakwood, the least you could have done was dressed for it.' The stern-faced woman said crossly.

'Witch Finder General, I am sorry.' The Target replied in a sweet and silky voice. 'I'm about to get into the bath you see, so I thought it was best to get ready as the two appointments overlapped.'

'What do you want Lady Oakwood?'

'Is that any way to speak to an old friend.'

'An old friend who is costing me time, resources and manpower.'

'Now, now Delphine. You know as well as I there is a killer on the loose, what if he works for the Demon.' The Target sounded worried.

'Lady Oakwood, I insist you refer to me by my title when we have official conversations.'

'As you command, Witch Finder General.'

'Now, this situation you have yourself in, is your own doing. You are the one who made the contract with the Demon. You are the one who has asked for our protection, and out of respect for our father's friendship, I have agreed. The Witch Hunters though are not a private security force, and the killer you have mentioned is on our radar. The marks are too similar to reports we have had in Gaia about...certain undesirables. Still, I doubt one of those things could have gotten through a gate, without us knowing.' Explained the Witch Finder General.

'Are you sure these wards of yours will work.' The Target asked.

'Your contract was up four days ago, in that time you have remained in one place and still live. Do you need more reassurance?'

'So, I am to stay here forever. What about my career?'

'Your career is over, Lady Oakwood, and as you know, it should have never begun in the first place. That is all the time I have for this meeting, until next time.'

'But wait...' The Target said, but the mirror turned back to normal and showed the reflection of the fraudulent Diva.

Sighing, the Target slipped out of her robe and stood naked before the mirror. Then Dorian saw May-Hem's mark in the centre of Lady Oakwood's back. His own mark began to itch, so he crept into the room as quietly as he could. Then Dorian made his way over to the target.

Lady Oakwood stood still all of the sudden and then her shoulders sagged.

The Soho Ripper

'Of course.' She said in a mournful voice. 'How simple.' The Diva turned and looked Dorian directly in the face.

Her body was smooth and pleasantly curved at the hips. Her breasts were full, and her nipples stood to attention as the breeze from the window hit them. Curled golden locks cascaded over her shoulders and down her back.

'Good evening, Lady Oakwood.' Dorian heard himself say with a calm he did not feel.

'You are his newest pet, are you. You are marked like me, I can tell. So, what did he offer you in exchange for this little task?' Lady Oakwood spoke calmly, but Dorian could see the fear in her eyes.

'He gave me a second chance at life.' Dorian admitted.

'For which, you are clearly prepared to do anything.' A tear formed under the Lady's eye. 'I guess that is more noble than giving up your unborn child for the voice of an angel.'

'Your unborn child?' Dorian was horrified.

'Oh yes, I had always wanted to be a singer, ever since I was a little girl and in my teens, I followed around some punk singer. He got me pregnant; I thought my life was over. Then May-Hem appeared to me, or maybe I summoned him. He told me my child would be the greatest Opera Singer of her generation but said that fame could be mine, all I had to do, was give him the child I didn't want.'

'And you signed the contract without a second thought.' Said May-Hem in his bemused voice.

'May-Hem!' Lady Oakwood gasped.

'I thought you said you couldn't get in here.' Dorian said annoyed.

'Oh, I couldn't,' May-Hem admitted, 'but you brought me in, disguised as a letter.'

'Guards!' Lady Oakwood shouted.

The door to the chamber burst open, but before the Witch Hunter could fully enter the room, May-Hem clicked his fingers. At once time stopped. Not for Dorian or May-Hem or even Lady Oakwood, but the door and the Witch Hunter pushing it open were frozen in time.

'What did you do?' Dorian asked, going over to the door and seeing the Witch Hunter frozen completely and midway to pulling out a pistol.

'Just a bit of time manipulation.' May-Hem said causally as if anyone could do it.

'Oh, right.' Dorian said, thinking about everything that had recently happened to him. So, time control was real too, why not.

'Please, I will give you anything you want!' Lady Oakwood begged.

'You have nothing left to give, my dear.' May-Hem took Lady Oakwood's cheek roughly by one hand and then pushed her to the bed. 'Come now, Dorian, I am sure you are thirsty.'

Dorian shook his head. He was thirsty, but he wanted nothing more to do with this. He didn't want the blood of this wretched creature.

'No?' May-Hem asked dramatically. 'Well suit yourself.' May-Hem turned back to Lady Oakwood and gave her a naughty smile. 'I guess you are all mine.' May-Hem held up a sheet of parchment before Lady Oakwood. 'Lady Oakwood, I gave you what you wished and waited ten years. Now, slightly overdue, I hold our contract fulfilled.' The parchment in his hand caught fire and burnt away.

'No, no! Please! No!' Lady Oakwood tried to crawl away on the bed.

'Your soul is mine.' May-Hem said as he reached and plunged his hand into his victim's chest.

As he pulled it out again, May-Hem took with him a glowing sphere of light. Before Dorian's eyes, Lady Oakwood turned to ash and crumbled away. May-Hem smiled down at his prize, before putting it up his sleeve.

'Another satisfied customer.' May-Hem chuckled. 'Until next time, Dorian, my dear.' Dorian looked up, but May-Hem was gone.

At once time started again and the Witch Hunter barged into the room.

'Lady...' He began. 'By God, what have you done you monster!'

The Witch Hunter lifted his pistol and fired at Dorian. Moving at an inhuman speed, Dorian dodged the shots. The gunfire caused alarms to go off throughout the building. Dorian heard footsteps and shouts from below.

Moving quickly, Dorian used his talons to disarm his attacker, by taking off his hands so red strike covered the silk wallpaper and velvet carpet. Then to stop him from knowing his face, Dorian took off his head in a single chopping motion. Then as the primal side of him took over once again, Dorian turned and hurdled himself out of the window.

In mid-air, Dorian felt his body shift and change. His shirt and jacket ripped as bony bat-like wings sprouted from his back. Laughing, Dorian found he could fly and so disappeared into the darkness above the clouds.

The Soho Ripper

Part Seven. Closure.

It had been two weeks since the death of Lady Penny Oakwood, and the murder had been blamed on the person the tabloids were calling *"The Soho Ripper"*.

It was now mid-October, and the few trees in London were all golden and brown with the autumn buzzing around them. People had started to dress warmer in with thick scarfs and big coats. This was Dorian's favourite time of year. Now he could wear coats, scarves and all his other favourite accessories.

Dorian strolled confidently down the streets of Soho, grinning to himself and filled with the blood of a lovely young couple. He had found them passed out in an alley the night before and could still taste the alcohol from their intoxicated veins. The two of them brought his total count to sixteen.

All seventeen kills were labelled as the work of the "Soho Ripper", including the death of Lady Oakwood. Dorian did not count her though in his personal list. May-Hem had ended her; Dorian had merely dispatched the guard.

The sense of guilt Dorian had at first felt with every kill was only a small ember compared to a bonfire of hunger, thirst, lust and desire. Being a Vampire was the best thing that had ever happened to him. He of course sometimes worried, about his changes and lack of control when the red thirst took over, but he was careful. There was also pig's blood in the fridge, combined now with cow and chicken's blood for variety.

One thing that upset him though, was now his reflection on any surface was completely gone. Not even the clothes he wore could be seen. He missed his face and found himself touching it often to remember his own beauty. Dorian was sure he had not been this vain in life, but now denied a reflection and even selfies, all he wanted was to see his face again.

To satisfy this yearning, he was now on his way to a portrait artist's home. He had made the appointment over the phone and paid a hefty deposit. Luckily Dorian always took all the cash from his victims. So, for the first time in his life he didn't need to worry about money. In the last week, he had "made" more cash than he normally did in a month. He was thinking about going part time. He had already asked for his shifts to be changed to the mornings instead of evenings.

Sunlight still bothered him but he found wearing gloves, sunglasses and a hat during the day kept him safe. Working during the day however, would keep him out of sunlight and not needing to sleep, he could hunt at night.

Noticing how the sunlight part of the legend only seemed to be half true, Dorian had visited a

The Soho Ripper

supermarket and nervously picked up some garlic. Nothing happened, so he sniffed it. It smelt revolting but did not cause him any discomfort.

Dorian also discovered he had no trouble with crucifixes and he didn't catch fire when he stepped into Saint Paul's Church, off Covent Garden. He did imagine how a wooden stake through the chest would kill him though, but he doubted he would come across any of those anytime soon. Would a bullet harm him, though? Dorian didn't want to find out.

Reaching the artist's building on Maiden Lane, Dorian buzzed and was let in. Climbing to the top of the stairs, Dorian found the door to flat fifteen wide open. Inside was a large attic studio apartment with a row of floor to ceiling windows.

Oil portraits hung on every wall. They varied from images of famous historical figures and modern celebrities to ordinary people on the street. By the window was a blank canvas on an easel. As Dorian walked in he came face to face with the artist.

If there was a stereotype for a fancy oil painter, this man was not it. The man in front of him was as skinny as a cocaine addict, with yellow teeth, bloodshot eyes and a half pink and half blue Faux Hawk haircut. The style put Dorian in mind of an extravagant chicken. Coupled with the stretched lobe piercings in each ear, a bull ring and spider bite lip piercings, Dorian wondered if he was in the right place. The apparent artist wore a long grey t-shirt and jean so tight they were practically leggings.

'Are you...' Dorian began but was interrupted.

'I am Diego.' The Artist said in a warm Spanish accent.

'Oh good.' Dorian put on a fake smile.

'So, you are here to be captured in time. To have your youth and beauty frozen forever.' Dorian just nodded. 'Then please step right ahead, and we shall begin. I shall take some sketches first and then paint.'

'I forgot to ask on the phone, how long does the whole process take?' Dorian said, taking off his gloves, coat, scarf and hat.

'Put your coat back on.' Diego ordered. 'It defines you well, I think. The overcoat works with your sharp cheekbones.'

'Thank you.' Dorian this time smiled for real as he put his coat back on.

'The process, as you ask, can take up to three months. We shall sketch today and meet once a week to paint.' Diego explained.

Dorian's smiled faded. 'Three months, no that won't do at all. Is there no way you can do it faster?'

'You cannot rush art.' Diego said defensively. 'Besides, I have other projects and other clients.'

The Soho Ripper

'No, Diego you misunderstood my question. Let me rephrase, how much to have it done before Halloween?'

'It is not a question of money.'

'My dear fellow,' Dorian chimed, 'everything is a question of money. So, let's say I pay double your asking price.'

Diego looked shocked. 'Double.'

'And I can pay you in advanced.' Dorian said pulling out his cash-filled wallet.

'You have yourself a deal.' Diego said greedily, eyeing the crisp notes sticking out between the leather.

With the sketches done for the day, Dorian decided to wander the streets of Soho. There were fewer people about than usual. Passing the alley where he had finished off Jade, Dorian saw a large flower memorial for the woman. Nearby a pop-up flower market had appeared. Seeing the unseasonal blooms, Dorian found himself wanting to show his respect.

Knowing Jade, probably better than any other person, Dorian decided to buy a single white rose. White roses had been her favourite, but from what he could see, there seemed to be none in the memorial.

Paying for the overpriced rose, Dorian turned and then marched up to the memorial. He walked between the stacks of flowers to the spot where Jade had died. Broken police tape surrounded the area and circled by a wreath of white roses, was a picture of Jade. Someone did know her after all. Carefully Dorian put the rose down on the spot he had ended her life, and then quietly he turned to walk away.

'A white rose.' Said a woman who was watching him in the mouth of the alley. Dorian recognised her at once. It was Bridget, Jade's best friend. 'You must have known her well, or it was a lucky guess.' Bridget spoke in a soft and sweet voice.

'I only met her the once, but she told me they were her favourite flower. You must be Bridget. She told me about you too, and described you perfectly.' Dorian lied.

'It was good of you to remember, and for you to pay your respects.' Bridget said.

'I am guessing you got the wreath.'

Bridget nodded. 'It was the least I could do for her.'

'Well, I wish you a good day.' Dorian gave her a nod and started to walk away.

'Sorry, I didn't get your name.'

'Dorian Winters.' Dorian heard himself say. Why didn't he lie?

'Dorian, that is a very traditional name.' Bridget said.

The Soho Ripper

'My mother is a huge fan of Oscar Wilde.'
Dorian said playfully.

'Oh yes, I do love that book. Do you plan on
being forever young and beautiful?'

'As a matter of fact, I have an artist painting a
portrait of me at the moment.' Dorian chuckled to
himself, only just realising the connection. 'It is a
gift for my mother.' He added in a quick lie.

'What will age though, you or the painting?'
Bridget almost smiled.

'Hopefully neither.'

'Nice to meet you, Dorian.'

'Bridget, I know we have only just met,'
Dorian heard himself say, 'but can I treat you to a
coffee? A quick drink to Jade, as it were.'

'I'd like that.'

Finding a little Hipster coffee shop, Dorian treated
Bridget to a warm glass of pumpkin spiced latte.
Dorian got himself a cup of black coffee for
appearance sake and pretended to sip it as he cooled
down. Luckily Bridget did not notice as she chatted
away about her life and Jade.

There were a few tears, a lot of happy memories
and some hearty laughs. Even though Dorian had
pushed out Jade's memories, as he had watched
them all he still remembered that experience. It was
strange to hear someone explain to him memories

he had watched, almost like listening to someone describe a film.

After their coffee, Dorian found himself walking through Soho Square, arm in arm, with Bridget. He wasn't entirely sure what he was doing with this woman, but he found he was enjoying himself.

'Oh, Dorian,' Bridget said between laughs, 'you have no idea how badly I needed a day like today. It has been so stressful, and with most of my family in New Zealand, I've had no one to talk to. You are a Godsend.'

'I wouldn't say God has anything to do with this.' Dorian said, glancing at Saint Patrick's Church.

Soho Square had a few people milling about on their lunch breaks, but it was also strangely quiet. The mock Tudor building ahead of them, which Dorian had always thought of as Shakespeare's House, had been plastered with posters. Glancing at them, Dorian saw the same image a hundred times bearing the legend, "Ripper Party This Halloween Soho Square." The image showed the popular image of Jack the Ripper as a Victorian gentleman with a bloody knife and a corpse at his feet.

'Disgusting.' Bridget said. 'People trying to profit from that monster's crimes.'

'Yes, very distasteful.' Dorian said.

The Soho Ripper

'Anyway,' Bridget said, pulling away from Dorian, 'I really must be off.'

'Let me walk you home.' Dorian said. 'I know it's the middle of the day, but I don't like the idea of you walking on your own.'

'You are sweet, but I'd rather be on my own for a bit.'

'Are you sure?'

'I am. Thank you for today, Dorian. It was nice to meet you.'

As Bridget walked away, Dorian watched her. He was hungry. The red thirst was in him. It was becoming more frequent, Dorian guessed he should worry about that, but at the moment he just wanted his next meal.

One thing Dorian had learnt, while walking along the rooftops, was so few people looked up. Walking above people was almost as good as willing himself unseen. It was very strange to think he could wander confidently, virtually anywhere and not worry about being seen or noticed.

With this confidence, Dorian stalked Bridget. She walked slowly heading down the less busy streets but avoiding the alleys. Small wonder considering what had happened to her best friend. Then Dorian had a sudden spark of cruel inspiration.

Joseph Willoughby-Rainsford

Bridget sauntered towards to her flat. She felt lucky to have met Dorian today, but there was something about him which made her feel uneasy. She couldn't quite put her finger on it, but the young man just seemed off.

Thinking about it, he reminded her of Jade's ex-boyfriend. He had been a high functioning alcoholic and so appeared healthy at first, but there was always the underlining thirst. Bridget hoped the young man wasn't too fond of the drink.

'Bridget!' A familiar voice called. The voice sounded in pain and sent a chill down her spine.

It couldn't be. Could it?

'Help me!' The voice called again.

It was. It had to be! It was Jade.

Bridget ran down the alleyway calling out. 'Jade! Jade, where are you?'

The alley was long and narrow and took her well away from the quiet road behind her. With the old brick buildings looming above her and seeming to lean toward each other, there was only a little light in the alley.

Turning a corner, Bridget found herself at a dead end. She looked around frantically, but there was no sign of her departed friend. Of course, there wasn't. It had been a trick of the wind or her mind or both she guessed.

The Soho Ripper

Tears rolled down her face as she turned and then jumped. There was a figure behind her. As he stepped into the lights, her heart soared.

'Dorian!' Bridget felt a moment of relief but then saw the look on his face. It was pure hunger. The look of a predator eying its prey. 'You're the Ripper!'

'I do not like that name. It is so overused.' Dorian sighed. 'The Yorkshire Ripper, the Blackout Ripper and of course the infamous Jack, and now apparently, me.'

'Why...' Bridget croaked.

'Because you are just food.' Dorian said as he grabbed her with inhuman strength and pulled her neck to his opening mouth.

Feeling the blood flowing his system and mixing with his own, Dorian smiled to him. He had left Bridget in a worse state than he had Jade. Slicing her to pieces of human sushi. He did this to hide the distinctive marks left on her but also because it had become his calling card.
There was two-hundred and fifty-eight pounds in her purse, so the coffee was more than paid for.

Using his rooftop parade, Dorian got as far away from the area as he could. He had no idea how long it would be until the body was found, but he didn't want to risk being found in the area. Dorian

Joseph Willoughby-Rainsford

ended up on the roof of the British Museum and
relaxed on the dome.

The Soho Ripper

Part Eight. Another Predator.

The young man in his arms struggled. Holding him
as close as a lover, Dorian sucked out his delicious
life energy.

His eighteenth victim was a twenty-year-old
hazel eyed beauty from Wales. Dorian had picked
him up between clubs and slowly guided him into
the graveyard at Saint Giles-in-the-Fields, saying
there was a quiet spot they could enjoy themselves.

Some of the newspaper's now thought there was
more than one killer. They said there had been too
many murders in such a short space of time and
nothing really to connect them. Another theory
attributed the deaths to gangs or some sort of Blood
Cult. Apparently two days on, Bridget's body still
had not been found.

As the boy in his arms let out his last gasp of
life, Dorian let go of him. The corpse dropped to the
dirt with a thud. Looking down at the lovely face,
Dorian gently closed the eyelids. Searching the
pockets, he found a "grand total" of five pounds.
'Five pounds! Really? Is that really all you have.
Oh, how disappointing.' Dorian glared.
He picked up the body of the youth. In anger, he
began to lash away. So, concentrated was he on
ruining this perfect young body, Dorian did not
notice the warning his ears gave him.

'Fuck! It's the Ripper!' Shouted a voice.

Joseph Willoughby-Rainsford

Turning in startlement, Dorian saw the two-young woman aiming their camera phones at him. The light of their torches lit Dorian's face. Hearing himself roar at them, Dorian turned and ran into the darkness.

He heard shouts and screams behind him as he disappeared onto a roof.

The next morning while Dorian got ready for his new early shift, Phil watched the morning news.

'There's been two more!' Phil called from the sofa.

Sorting out his tie Dorian replied. 'Two what?'

'What do you mean two what?' Phil shouted back. 'Murders of course. I swear Dorian; you are in your own world these days.'

'Haven't they caught the villain yet?' Dorian asked.

'Of course not.' Phil replied. 'He got the is she the best friend of that first woman and some young gay guy. You should start avoiding the clubs.'

'The clubs are my life.' Dorian joked.

'Yes, and they might be your death too.' Phil replied.

'I'm sure I have nothing to worry about.'

Dorian walked out of his room and put on his coat. Phil and Leroy were watching the television. Leroy was dressed in his running gear and about to put his headphones in.

The Soho Ripper

'Seriously, Dorian you do need to be careful.' Leroy said, giving him a look.

'I'll be fine. See you later.' Dorian nodded to the pair.

'Wait, Dorian.' Phil said suddenly. 'There's a vigil tonight for the victims in Soho Square. You should come with Leroy and me.'

'Why?' Dorian looked at Phil with a genuinely puzzled expression.

'Why!' Phil looked crestfallen. 'Solitary, compassion, empathy and respect. Where is your sense of community?'

'Community...and what community would this be?' Dorian allowed anger to enter his tone.

'The L.G.B.T.Q community!' Phil all but shouted.

Dorian let out a hollow laugh. He couldn't help himself. Then he looked at Phil and saw he was serious and then angering once more Dorian snapped, 'There is no L.G.B.T.Q community! There is only a bunch of self-righteous, self-involved, alcoholic and drug addicted media and selfie whores, mixed together in a shallow drunken stupor of vanity and lust. The idea that any of them really care for anyone else is laughable at best. They will mourn for the victims because it looks good in a FaceSpace post and pose for photos with the community, pouting and pulling 'my dog just died face', to gain more followers. The only time they

72

will really care is the moment the ripper cuts out their black, shrivelled hearts.'

With that Dorian left the apartment, slamming the door closed.

After work, Dorian took his rooftop path back toward Covent Garden. During his alone time above the streets, Dorian thought about the night before. He had been seen! That was very careless of him. It was only money he was angry about. Only money! Why had he gotten so angry? The boy had given Dorian his whole life.

Coming to a complete stop, Dorian leant against a chimney. He needed to calm down and concentrate. He had an appointment to go to, and he had nothing to worry about. There was no way the cameras of those girls would have caught him, and in the suddenness of the moment, they wouldn't have been able to see his face. Had his face changed shape? If so then he didn't have anything to worry about at all. No, that wasn't true. There were the Witch Hunters.

Those strangely dressed and well-armed men. They seemed to know something about the strange world Dorian had fallen into. Fallen into, was that really the case? There was no doubt Dorian had now embraced his changes. He couldn't even hear his inner moral compass anymore.

'Stop it, Dorian!' He said out loud.

The Soho Ripper

Suddenly something caught his attention. Something his senses had never picked up on before. It was nearby. The primal part of him moved in the dark shadows of his mind. This was another predator. Not one of his kind, but something far older and possibly more dangerous.

With a thrill of excitement, Dorian rushed off towards a fight. In the past, before his change, Dorian shrunk from confrontation, but now this was his territory. London was his. He was the King of the Night, the Prince of Shadows and wouldn't let this thing, whatever it was, take from his prey.

Running at full speed, Dorian jumped from roof top to roof top. He leapt over Oxford Street and landed on the side of the Jack Ellis department store so hard the glass cracked. He crawled quickly to the roof and then continued to run and jump.

Reaching Manchester Square, Dorian circled it and leapt onto the tiled roof of Hertford House. One of the tiles came loose and fell to the ground causing someone to scream, but Dorian kept moving.

Less than two minutes later Dorian dropped into an untidy backstreet near a clock repair shop. By his feet was a newspaper article about him. Dorian glanced at it then he suddenly heard shouting from the clock repair shop. That was the place his target was. Dorian stepped forward when there was an almost blinding green flash.

Joseph Willoughby-Rainsford

Unable to see for a few seconds Dorian stumbled as he blinked. There was the twinkle of a bell ringing as the door to the shop opened. Not able to see, Dorian's other sense told him where his target was.
Tick.

Leaping, Dorian went to tackle the black shape before him.
Tick.

It was fast. Dorian hit the ground. He rolled and moved away just in time to avoid a blade.
Tick.

Getting to his feet, Dorian was now able to see slightly better. The creature before him had the shape of a man, but Dorian knew it was no human. A human corpse or a combination of bodies said his nose. A human body filled with clockwork cogs and gears said his ears. Inside all of that, though was something else, something powerful said a sense which worked beyond the physical world.
Tick.

The figure turned away and began to run.
Tick.

Dorian followed as fast as he could. When he was about to reach the creature, he stretched out his arm. His hand turned into claws, and he was going to attack. The figure spun on his feet, and a bronze blade appeared from nowhere.
Tick.

The Soho Ripper

The blade slice Dorian's arm off. The arm flew
away in a spurt of blood and dissolved into ash
before it hit the floor.
Tick.

In shock, Dorian screamed. The human part of
him wanted to run and escape, but the primal side of
him took full control.
Tick.

Brand new black leather shoes burst apart as
Dorian's feet shifted into spiked weapons. Then
Dorian felt his body jump and kick out. His taloned
foot was brought down across the figure's body. His
foot ripped through a trench coat and into rotten
flesh.
Tick.

As the figure reeled back, Dorian felt his fist
punch right through its chest. Pieces of rotten flesh,
oozing black oil and bronze gears and cogs burst
out of the creatures back.
Tick.

'Got ya!' Dorian snarled.
Tick.

Then the creature pulled back and slashed his
sword towards Dorian's other arm. Pulling his arm
out and up, Dorian saw the creature's shoulder part
from its neck. The sword moved down, and Dorian
felt pain as both of his legs disappeared. They
dissolved into ash as Dorian fell to the ground.
Tick.

Joseph Willoughby-Rainsford

Sprouting wings out of his back, Dorian flapped wildly to get away from this creature. Even his primal side knew he was beaten and the instinct to survive took over. Dorian watched the strange figure keep an eye on him as he flew away.

Phil was leaning back on the sofa, dressed only in his boxers. His belly bulged over the elastic waistband, as he sat back and enjoyed some pizza. He had an interview later for a bar position that evening, but he wouldn't worry about getting ready before his roommates got home.

Flicking through the channels, Phil thought about going into Dorian's room to borrow his laptop. He wasn't sure how Dorian would react to this, though. His friend had changed recently. The warm and friendly Dorian had been replaced with someone Phil no longer felt he knew.

The whole world seemed to be going upside down. Phil didn't usually follow the news, but this serial killer business and whatever was going on across the Atlantic with the new President was in his opinion "messed up".

A smash of glass brought Phil back to the here and now. The sound had come from Dorian's room. Getting up, Phil opened the door and peered in. He wondered if some kid had thrown a brick, or maybe one of Dorian's scorned lovers.

The Soho Ripper

The whole window was entirely smashed with glass scattered around the room. There was a trail of blood from the window, across the floor to the bed. Laying on the sheets was a huddled figure. Blood was everywhere. The huddle was a mess of trembling limps.

Screaming, Phil fell over backwards and hit his head on Dorian's chest of draws. The horrific shape moved like a wounded spider towards him across the bed. A face peered out at Phil from beneath a mane of bristly black hair.

'Dorian!' Phil gasped, recognising his friend's pale, gaunt features underneath the blood and filth.

'I...need...I...need...' Dorian said quickly.

Getting a good look at him now, Phil saw his friend had lost an arm and both of his legs but seemed to have great leathery wings sprouting from his back.

'1 will call an ambulance.' Phil said, reaching for his phone.

Opening his hand, Dorian dropped a few broken gears covered in black goo onto his bed. Phil shivered as Dorian placed his hand on his shoulder.

'I...need...' Dorian repeated in a whisper.

'What do you need, mate?' Phil said leaning in.

Dorian's face was by Phil's neck. With the wounded man so close to him, Phil could feel his breath. It was cold like his touch.

'Blood.' Dorian whispered into Phil's ear.

Joseph Willoughby-Rainsford

Phil frowned in confusion and then let out a scream of pain as fangs ripped into his neck.

Laying in a mixture of his own and Phil's blood, Dorian felt his arm and legs regrowing. It was an amazing, but horribly painful experience as bone and muscle grew out of his stumps. A thin layer of skin began to form over each new limb.

The process seemed to take ours and used up so much of Dorian's strength and all of Phil's. His roommate was empty now and slumped at the end of Dorian's bed. With not a single drop of blood inside, Phil had shrivelled. Dull grey skin stuck tightly to his bones and deflated muscles.

During the healing process, Dorian's body brought in his wings and retook full human form. With what strength he had, Dorian pushed Phil's corpse away. With a sickening hollow thud, the body hit the wooden floor.

Getting up, Dorian headed straight to the shower. He put the water on the coldest setting and leant his face against the tiles letting the water pour all over him. He was probably in the shower for more than an hour when he heard the front door to the flat open.

'Funny,' Dorian heard Leroy say, 'the Televisions on, where's Phil.'

'Is that not him in Dorian's room.' Lauren giggled.

The Soho Ripper

'The shower is on, Phil must have passed out after sex, and Dorian is washing him off.'

'Gross. Dorian would never.'

'Dorian has a few times. I've heard them.'

No longer leaning in the shower, Dorian felt his fangs and fingers growing in length.

'Leroy!' Lauren's voice sounded shrill. 'There's blood on the floor. Lots of blood.'

There were more footsteps. Dorian knew both Leroy and Lauren were entering his room.

'Oh, my God!' Lauren screamed.

'Phil!' Leroy shouted.

In a flash, Dorian smashed through the bathroom door and charged into his bedroom. Leroy and Lauren jumped, and Dorian stood naked and dripping in the doorway. Leroy's phone was half way to his ear. In a single movement, Dorian swiped it out of Leroy's hand, so it shattered on the floor.

'Dorian! What are you doing? What's wrong with your face?' Leroy asked, standing protectively in front of Lauren.

'You're the Ripper!' Lauren pointed a finger.

In a movement, too fast for either Lauren or Leroy to see Dorian was passed them and behind Lauren. Taking Lauren by the throat, he held her like a ragdoll and savaged her throat. Feeling Lauren struggle and hearing her whimper, Dorian watched as Leroy stared at the scene in stunned horror.

Lauren's free hand reached up and tried to scratch at Dorian's face, but after a second it fell limp. There was no sound as Lauren's heartbeat stopped.

'Such a pity.' A soft voice said through Dorian. 'She died so quickly and put up no fight. She must have had a weak heart.'

'You bastard!' Leroy raised his fists and ran at Dorian.

Dropping Lauren's lifeless form to the floor, Dorian readied himself for Leroy's punch. The fist came flying towards him and Dorian span out of its way. Bringing his hands around; Dorian went to strike Leroy on the back of the head.

Then there was the sound of breaking wood as the front door was kicked in. Dorian peered back. His senses had detected people coming up the stairs, but he'd assumed they were other tenants of the building. Looking back, Dorian saw four Witch Hunters. All their pistols aimed at him.

Pain had happened.

It was an itching burning pain. The pistols of the Witch Hunter's contained silver bullets. Dorian had quickly discovered silver bullets hurt him badly.

Now Dorian was on his knees with two Witch Hunter's aiming their guns at him. Scarves and hoods covered their faces. Leroy had been sat on the sofa and given a box of tissues.

'Why don't you just kill me and get it over with?' Dorian growled.

'Because,' Said a stern voice Dorian knew, 'we are here to make you a deal, Dorian Winters, or should I say the Soho Ripper.'

Dorian looked up and saw an older woman in a grey pant suit. She had a sword on her hip with a golden hilt. It was the stern-faced woman from Lady Oakwood's mirror. The Witch Finder General.

'So, you know who I am.' Dorian smirked.

'We know who you were and what you have become. I must admit you did have us puzzled for a while. A vampire, but not one who had come through any gate.' The Witch Finder General said. 'But you gave yourself away by your hunting habits, still, once we knew a Vampire was in London, the question remained, who was it.'

'How did you find me?' Dorian asked, with real curiosity.

'The gears you ripped out of the Ticker's chest. We can track them when they are this close to our base of operations.' Another Witch Hunter explained.

'Thank you, Paladin Michael.' The Witch Finder General nodded to the Witch Hunter by Leroy.

'What is the Ticker?' Dorian questioned.

Joseph Willoughby-Rainsford

'The Creature you fought today.' The Witch Finder General explained.

'So, you mentioned a deal?' Dorian asked.

'You need to kill that monster! He killed Lauren!' Leroy cried out.

'Shut it, frog.' Paladin Michael slapped Leroy round the back of the head.

'Yes, there is a deal on the table. You see, we want to capture the Ticker. As you are the first person in over a hundred years to harm it. You will accompany a group of my finest Hunters, and together you will bring the Ticker in.' The Witch Finder General said.

'What do I get out of this?' Dorian asked.

'We don't kill you now.'

'I see, and what about after?'

'A report is already on its way to the police. It states how Dorian Winters was the Soho Ripper but killed himself by jumping in front of a train. This has all been taken care of. Officially, Dorian, you are now dead.' The Witch Finder General explained calmly as if she was discussing the weather. 'So after, Dorian, you will need to stay useful.'

'Who are you people?'

'We are the Witch Hunters. Protectors of Earth against the unholy forces of Gaia.' The Witch Finder General stated proudly.

The Soho Ripper

'I see.' Dorian said. 'Well I am still a little under the weather at present, so I will need a little bit of time to rest and recuperate.'

The Witch Finder General moved closer and peered directly into Dorian's face. 'I wonder.' She said. 'How much of you is the man you used to be and how much is the monster?'

'I'd say I take no pleasure in what I have become, but that would be an utter lie.'

'Do we have a deal?'

'What choice do I have?'

'None.'

'Then I guess, I'm your servant.'

'Good.' The Witch Finder General turned and looked at Paladin Michael. 'Michael, no witnesses.'

'Yes, my Lady.' Michael said as he grabbed Leroy and threw him to Dorian. 'Vampire, eat.'

Hesitating for a second, Dorian looked from Leroy's startled face to the Witch Hunters.

'Seriously?' He asked.

'The police reports have listed all your roommates as your final victims.'

Looking down at Leroy, Dorian saw the look of anger and defiance in his former friend's eyes. This man was his friend no longer; he was just food now. A source of nutrition and strength.

Lowering himself to Leroy's neck, the last human part of Dorian said, 'I'm sorry.' Before giving into the urge and biting.

Joseph Willoughby-Rainsford

Part Nine. The Ticker.

The helicopter flew over the sleeping London.

Having never been in a chopper before, Dorian found the experience rather enjoyable, despite the circumstance he found himself in. The Witch Hunter's had allowed him time to change as they dealt with the bodies of Phil, Lauren and Leroy. Making them appear as mangled as Dorian's former victims.

No longer able to feel the cold, Dorian had decided to wear light and tight fitting black gym wear under his new black trench coat. He'd not bothered with shoes as they would only get in the way.

Before leaving his flat for the last time, the Witch Hunter's had put a collar-shaped device around his neck as if he was a dog.

'It's a tracking device, and it's loaded with liquid silver.' Paladin Michael explained. 'If you try anything, it will go off, and you'll be melting into ash before you can get your fang's out.'

'Good to know.' Dorian growled.

Now, Dorian and five Witch Hunters were riding in the military issue helicopter. It was strange to see London from so high up and know it was no longer his home. The lights of the urban sprawl seemed faded beneath the wispy cloud.

The Soho Ripper

Then Dorian's sense twitched. The Ticker was nearby. He could feel it. Only a few miles away, and at the speed the Helicopter flew he'd be there in no time.

'You are going in first.' Explained Paladin Michael. Like his companions, he'd changed from his long brown leathers into a suit of light black leather and plate armour. To Dorian, they all looked like futuristic knights, with their swords, pistols and electronic visors. 'Once on the ground, you are to track down the Ticker and engage. Do not let it escape. Keep its concentration on you.'

'What will you be doing?' Dorian asked.

'My men and I shall be getting into position to capture the creature. Disarm it if you can but be careful of its built-in sword.' Michael continued.

'Oh, don't worry. I don't plan on losing any limbs this time.' Dorian grinned.

They were directly above the Ticker now. Dorian didn't need the fact the helicopter had stopped to tell him that. Paladin Michael's stood up and opened the side hatch.

'It's a good thing I had custom made clothes tailored for wing holes.' Dorian stated as he got up and walked to the edge.

'Good hunting.' Said, Michael.

Dorian gave him a mock salute and then allowed gravity to take him. The wind howled in his ears as Dorian fell through the sky. Angling his body, Dorian allowed himself to plummet for some time before extending his wings. As he opened them, the wind caught them at once, and Dorian began to glide. He flew in lazy circles around an old church.

Looking down, Dorian saw they were not over London anymore but in the countryside somewhere. Not too far off though as Dorian could see London to the south. There was a sleepy village down the hill from the church, an old wood and then miles and miles of farmland.

Considering the possible entrances to the building, Dorian decided he would go through the main doors. He wanted to confront the Ticker as a proud hunter, not a sneaking assassin. Swooping close to the ground, Dorian retracted his wings and then landed neatly on the gravel path leading to the church entrance.

With his perfect night vision, Dorian saw the doors of the church were wide open. There was a scent of decay in the air and something sweeter. Fresh blood. The Ticker was close, and it seemed he had found a victim. Dorian wondered if it ate humans or drank their blood as he did.

'Well, well Dorian,' said May-Hem, 'working for the enemy now, are we?'
May-Hem was calmly sat on a gravestone. His legs crossed as he picked at his sharp teeth with a

dagger. On his knee was a jar glowing with an inner whirling mist.

'Not really been given much choice.' Dorian said, coolly.

'Well, you have got yourself in a spot of bother and now are about to come face to face with one of the most dangerous creatures in this world.' May-Hem said, seeming to enjoy the moment.

'Any advice, to deal with this Ticker.' Dorian asked.

'Ticker?' May-Hem laughed. 'Is that what they call him. His name, or at least what he is known as where we come from is Mr Tick. As for advice, here is some for free, don't die.'

'You know I feel this second chance you gave me wasn't worth it. I've lost everything.' Dorian sneered.

'Is that really how you feel?' May-Hem grinned devilishly.

'You know, I feel like that is how I should feel, but in truth, I cannot help being grateful to you.' Dorian admitted.

'What a kind thing to say. Well Dorian, as I find myself liking you, despite your many and evident flaws, I shall grant you one answer for information, completely free of charge.'

'Just one...well. Tell me, what are you?'

'Is that what you really want to know.' May-Hem's eyes narrowed.

'Yes.'

'No, you really don't, but as that was your question, I shall be true to my offer. I am what lays in the heart of all men, the soft touch of evil. I am desire. I am lust. I am the spirit of anger. I am the spark which ignites chaos. I am the harbinger of doom. I am the bane of your former race. I am a merchant of misery, and my currency is souls.' He patted the jar. 'Do you remember when you signed the contract, I told you I'd take one thing from each of your victims. Well as you have drunk from their life-force, I have taken their souls. These I shall feast upon, and so my power shall increase.'

As he spoke, May-Hem's feature grew more fiendish. His cheeks hollowed. Dark red veins appeared across his face. His eyes burned with an inner fire. The appearance was demonic.

'Are you a demon?' Dorian asked backing away.

'I said one answer.' May-Hem's voice was deeper.

Jumping off the gravestone, May-Hem began to stroll off with his jar while whistling an eerie tune. The darkness seemed to surround May-Hem quickly, and then he was gone.

Pushing his feelings of unease away, Dorian walked forward and entered the dim church. The door had

been smashed open. The splinters spread out across the entry way.
Tick.

A few candles flickered within the church, but for the most part, it was dark. Dorian though was able to see perfectly. All around him, he saw the pews facing the altar. By the altar was a hunched over figure. It was from there Dorian got the smell of decay mixed with fresh blood.
Tick.

The Ticker or Mr Tick was leaning over the corpse of a priest. With a steady hand, the creature was slicing off bits of skin and then sewing them to its own horrific body.
Tick.

What had once been the priest of this small church was now a bloodstained pile of meat and bones. Blood was sucked up from a tube which extended out of Mr Tick's chest and into the stomach of the priest.
Tick.

'How inelegant and disgusting.' Dorian said aloud.
Tick.

Mr Tick did not look up, but he spoke in a rough voice. 'Why do you hunt me. I mean you no harm, spawn of Dracula.'
Tick.

'You know I have never met this Dracula, so I wouldn't really call myself his spawn.' Dorian replied.

Tick.

'His scent is all over you. You are of his line, whether you know it or not. I am curious how you managed to also get trapped in this decaying world.'

Tick.

'I was born here.'

Tick.

Mr Tick looked up there and was about to speak, and then he grinned showing rotten teeth. 'Oh, May-Hem, of course. Of course.' The creature laughed. The sound was like a rusted engine trying to activate. 'He would want me out of the picture, oh how he has played the game. You don't even realise you are doing exactly what he wants.'

'I don't care if I am doing what he wants. Defeating you gets me what I want.'

Mr Tick stood up to his full height. Not wearing his coat, Dorian could see Mr Tick's body for what it was, a horrific mishmash of decaying corpses. There were still holes in his flesh, allowing Dorian to see into the ticking clockwork within.

A bronze sword was extended from each of Mr Tick's arms. The creature seemed to stretch out his arms and then slowly began to walk forward.

At the same time, Dorian allowed his hands and feet to change into clawed weapons. He felt his face change shape, and his fangs extend out of his widening jaw. Then the primal part of him twitched. Allowing it to take a small bit of control, Dorian felt long mandibles grow out of his shoulder blades and up over his shoulders.

Letting out a roar, Dorian charged at Mr Tick. The two creatures met in the centre of the church. Claws met swords in a clash of sparks. Both beasts moved as fast as they could. Dorian, found he was faster, but Mr Tick was stronger.

Slashing at one another, Dorian's talons pulled off strands of rotten flesh from across Mr Tick's body. Bits of the old skeleton and pieces of moving clockwork became visible. At the same time, Dorian felt the blades of his enemy lacerate his arms, legs and back.

With lightning quick reaction, Dorian brought one of his mandibles down. The razor-sharp point harpooned into Mr Tick's shoulder. The clockwork demon pulled back and brought back his arms around in complete circles, ripping apart his skin and muscles at the arm joints. The move allowed Mr Tick to slice off the mandible.

Dorian screamed out in an animal's howl of pain and jumped back. The chopped limb dissolved into ash, and Dorian felt his right stump twitch as what was left retracted into him. Then as Mr Tick tried to click his arms back into place, Dorian took his chance.

Joseph Willoughby-Rainsford

The vampire brought both of his clawed hands in close to Mr Tick and ripped into the creature's foul chest. A mixture of fresh and rotten blood, new and old skin, oil and gears flew in all directions. Dorian felt like a burrowing animal as he stripped away layer after layer of Mr Tick's foulness.

Then the clockwork demon let out a strange fizzing sound, and Dorian found himself pushed away by an invisible force. Flying backwards, Dorian smashed through a pillar. Trying to get back up Dorian found his legs were broken. He needed a minute or two for them to heal. Thinking and moving quickly, Dorian grabbed pieces of the broken stone and threw them one by one as Mr Tick walked towards him.

With a chest in ruins and dripping upon the cold stone floor, Mr Tick deflected the pieces of limestone with his spinning blades. Dorian kept throwing the pieces, but soon Mr Tick was on top of him. The creature brought down both of its weapons into Dorian's chest as he tried to crawl away. Then the creature lifted him up like a trophy. Dorian's blood dripped all over Mr Tick's face but unseen by the demon; Dorian held a piece of the pillar still.

Dorian brought down the jagged piece of rock. There was a sickening crunch as it smashed into Mr Tick's skull. Flesh ripped. Bone scattered. Brains burst. Mr Tick span and threw Dorian across the room to the altar. Dorian landed heavily on the remains of the priest. His hands slipped in the blood, and his cuts allowed the blood to flow in.

Then Dorian felt a strange connection to the corpse at his feet. He could sense all of the priest's blood. Not only the blood entering his system but the blood on the floor and the blood inside Mr Tick.

The clockwork demon stood in the middle of the church. Half of his skull had caved in. One of his eyes glowed green while the other hung out of his head. Where his brain should have been, was a grey mush oozing onto the floor. Beneath the thick pulp was a large amethyst held in place by a bronze wire frame.

Mr Tick stumbled for a moment and then righted himself and looked at Dorian who was crouched over the priest's dead form. Lifting up an arm, Dorian suddenly found his body grabbed by some sort of invisible hand. He was lifted off the ground as Mr Tick staggered towards him. The invisible hand holding Dorian squeezed. If he had been a human, his air would have been cut off, and his bones would have snapped. To Dorian the vampire, however, it was just a very uncomfortable experience as his body tried to resist the enormous amount of strength.

Dorian then closed his eyes, and within his mind, he saw the spider web-like network of blood. It glowed crimson in a sea of darkness. It started within the priest where it was small and flat but stretch up into a light network within Dorian and then across little islands of red it crisscrossed throughout Mr Tick's body. Dorian felt his mind travel through the blood taking control of the blood cells one by one. Then Dorian sent out a command through the blood.

Mr Tick stopped moving, and Dorian fell to the ground. As Dorian stood, he stretched out his arms like a puppeteer. Red droplets flew into the air and turned into fine threads from Dorian's fingers to the body of his enemy. The clockwork demon struggled against them, but Dorian held his ground and forced the demon into a kneeling position.

'Checkmate.' Dorian said and then began to laugh wildly.

As Dorian pulled his arms away from each other Mr Tock was ripped limb from limb. The creature's arms and legs flew up and landed on the floor and then his torso was sliced in two.

'That's enough Dorian.' Said Paladin Michael. 'Stop, or I'll activate your collar.'

Dorian allowed the blood to fall to the floor and stood still. As he watched from the altar, Witch Hunters rushed in and began to gather up the pieces of Mr Tick into different containers.

'You have done the Witch Hunter's a great service. So many have been killed to keep this creature functioning over the last one hundred and fifty years.' Michael was saying. 'We and all of

Earth are in your debt, and with these pieces, we may learn more about the magic of our enemy.'

'You are welcome,' Dorian said suspiciously, 'so now do you remove my collar and let me go free?'

More Witch Hunters entered the church. A lot more. These were all dressed in the traditional brown coats, and each held a rifle.

Paladin Michael lifted up a small device. The controls to the collar.

'For what it is worth I am sorry. You never asked for this, and it is not your fault the monster took control of your body.' Michael said as he went to click.

Using his new-found control over blood, Dorian allowed his blood to rip out of his neck and slice apart the collar. At the same moment, Michaels clicked the button. Sharp spike sprung out of the falling pieces of the collar and sprayed out liquid silver. Dorian stepped back quickly, so none of the shining liquid touched him.

'Men, open fire!' Michael shouted.

At once, the rifles were lifted and then began to spray volleys of silver bullets towards Dorian. Jumping into the air, Dorian allowed the inner beast to take over and found to his astonishment and delight that his body was dissolving into mist.

Letting out another wild laugh, Dorian whirled like a tornado of energy, blood and darkness. He exploded out of the roof of the church and expanded into the sky.

The Soho Ripper

Part Ten. The Reflection of Dorian Winters.

'I see.' The Witch Finder General said looking up from the report.

The Grand Master of the Witch Hunter's British Chapter sat at her mahogany desk within the confines of her office. From the grand windows behind her could be seen a vast open field surrounded by dense forest.

Before the red leather topped desk stood Paladin Michael, wearing his white dress uniform. The seal of the order hung around his neck and medals covered his chest. On his hip hung a gold-hilted ceremonial sword.

'A vampire so young should not have been able to use that kind of power.' The Witch Finder General said in a low voice. 'Clearly, we do not know as much about them as we thought.'

'There have been no attacks in his style at all in the United Kingdom since, my lady.' Michael said. 'My men continue to search, but there is no sign of him.'

'If we are lucky he was unable to reform and shall spend eternity as a cloud.' The Witch Finder General sighed. 'Never mind Michael, this is not a reflection on you. You did very well to capture the Ticker and control a dangerous situation. Your gamble paid off, and the Council is very pleased.'

'You gave the green light, my lady.'

'Indeed, but as you military types say; orders given by commanders, not on the ground are not worth shit.' The thin lips parted in a rare smile which lasted less than a second. 'His Lordship, the Witch Finder General from the United States, wants to promote you and make you his Lord Commander.'

'I would like to refuse his kind offer, my lady.'

'Why?'

'Permission to speak honestly, and off the record?'

'Granted.'

'I'd rather serve in heaven, than rule in hell, as it were.'

'How droll, but in the current climate, I fear you serve in hell nevertheless. I am glad you refused though, as I would hate to lose so fine a Hunter. While I cannot promote you to Lord Commander at present, be assured you are the only candidate I will consider when the time comes.'

'Your ladyship is too kind.'

'Now go, enjoy the ceremony being held in your honour. I have details to attend to.'

Paladin Michael bowed and then left the office. A few minutes later, the Witch Finder General stood up from her desk and strolled out of her office. She took a lift to a sub-basement, deep below the country estate, which served as Head Quarters to the British Chapter of the Witch Hunters.

The Soho Ripper

Down here the walls were modern and white. So, clean you could eat your dinner off them if gravity allowed it. Passing guards on duty who bowed to her, the Witch Finder General entered a large room. Within the chamber were rows of floor to ceiling tanks. Within each one were the captured, catalogued, studied and dissected remains of creatures from Gaia.

There were more than five-thousand specimens in various chambers throughout the compound. Walking over to a table in the middle of the room, the order's doctors greeted the Witch Finder General. Around the table were consoles and trays of equipment. Upon the table were the still-living remains of the Ticker.

'My lady, we are learning a lot.' Said one of the doctors. It is utterly fascinating, although it is clockwork, the body seems to be powered by this amethyst. I believe it is in there the actual creature is held captive.'

'Do you think we will be able to subjugate it?'

'Do you have plans, my lady?'

'One must always look ahead.'

'As you say. Well, in truth, I am not sure. These creatures as you know do serve humans in Gaia, but I am not certain how such an arrangement is...arranged.'

'Is there nothing in the Exiled Prince's journals.' The Witch Finder General asked.

Joseph Willoughby-Rainsford

'Nothing of use.' The Doctor admitted.

'Well, carry on Doctor, don't stop on my account.'

The Witch Finder General stepped back and watched as the scientists continued to pull apart the remains. The flesh was unstitched and separated. Each part was taken to be identified and studied. The gears were removed and cleaned, and in a nearby area, they were reassembled.

As the Witch Finder General watched, she thought about the Exiled Prince. It had been years since the two had last seen each other. At the time her father had been the Witch Finder General. Their father, she corrected herself, no matter what else he was Gareth Prince remained and would always be the brother of Witch Finder General Delphine Janet Prince.

Diego was not having a good day. Two of his appointments had cancelled last minute, and he was unsure about what to do with the painting in his studio. It had been a shock when Diego found out the very handsome young man he had been painting was the Soho Ripper.

All those murders and he had been in Diego's studio.

The portrait had been in his studio when a reporter came to do a puff piece on his work. The editorial then became a piece on Diego's apparent obsession with the Soho Ripper. Since then he'd been losing clients faster than he could snort up his favourite white powder.

The startlingly attractive oil painted features of Dorian Winters stared back at him as Diego sat. He probably should destroy it. It was unlikely the serial killer would be able to locate it, and nowhere would ever display it. Still, Diego hesitated. There were no two ways about it; this almost life-size portrait was the best work he had ever done. It had not only captured the beauty of what was an incredibly good-looking man, but it had also captured the darkness lurking in his heart and the hunger in his eyes. Seen from certain angles the portrait seemed to show a hellish demonic figure and not the confident young man. Diego was not sure how this had happened, he knew he hadn't meant to paint it that way.

During the week after he had met Dorian for the first time, Diego had spent ages pouring over his sketches and trying to do the man justice. It had become an obsession of his. He needed to impress this young man to give him all he could from his torn-up soul, and he had delivered.

When he saw the finished product after applying the final brush stroke, Diego had collapsed and began to weep. It had been later on the same day when he had seen the news report on Dorian.

Pondering on what to do with the painting, Diego wondered if putting it into storage until a museum or tourist trap about the young serial killer was made. Surely someone would try to make profit on this morbid subject. Goodness knew there were a few such locations in London dedicated to the macabre.

'It is stunning.' A voice said behind him.

Diego jumped and let out a cry of alarm. Turning he knocked over a small table and paint splashed onto the floor. Out of the shadowy corner of his studio, Dorian seemed to be appearing out of the darkness.

'My God!' Diego cursed before muttering a prayer in Spanish.

Walking up to the painting, Dorian looked at it and smiled. He was wearing a stylish long coat, black jeans and a white shirt. His hair had been changed since the last time Diego had seen it. Now he wore it with skin faded sides, and all oiled back from his widow's peak.

As Dorian reached the painting, he looked directly into it as if it was a person he was about to greet. Diego was frozen in astonished fear. He just watched as Dorian admired the painting. Then the serial killer looked at him and gave him a cheeky boyish grin.

'Do I really look like this?' He asked.

Diego just nodded, and Dorian turned back to the painting.

The Soho Ripper

'Oh,' he cooed, 'my image, how I have missed you.' Turning back to Diego, Dorian said. 'You have outdone yourself. Clearly, this is your best work, and I am not just saying that because it's a picture of me.'

'I agree.' Diego trembled.

Stretching out his arm, Dorian grabbed Diego by the shoulder and brought him closer. This surprised Diego as he thought he was too far for Dorian to reach. As the icy hand pulled him forward, he seemed to float instead of being dragged.

'Don't be afraid.' Dorian said.

Diego gasped in pain as he felt Dorian's lips close around his neck and two teeth prick his flesh. It was like having two injections at the same time. Then there was an almost orgasmic rush of pleasure as Dorian began to lick and suck.

'My...God...' Diego heard himself gasp.

Blood flowed through him, and his skinny jeans got tighter around his crotch as Diego pressed himself against the lean figure of Dorian. Then Diego began to feel dreamy and weak. Dorian's arm pressed against his back and held him in place.

Then Dorian brought his lips away from Diego's neck. His face was red with blood as he looked into the dim eyes of the artist. Still holding Diego up, Dorian slashed his wrist with his own nail and then brought the red flowing wound towards Diego's mouth.

'I offer you a second chance at life.' Dorian murmured.

Diego opened his mouth wide and began to lap up the blood flowing from Dorian's wound. It was a darker red than normal blood and sticky and thick. There was a sweet tang to it. Dorian groaned in pleasure.

Then Diego felt himself fall backwards as Dorian let go of him. Falling to the floor, Diego felt pain begin to burn its way through his veins.

'Am I dying?' He asked Dorian who was looking at the painting again.

'No.' Dorian smiled. 'You are being reborn.'

Moving with the grace of a hunting lion, Dorian lowered himself on top of Diego. With a wild strength, he ripped off the artist's shirt and jeans and then lowering himself, Dorian grabbed Diego's boxers with his teeth and pulled them down. As he moved, Dorian's own clothes seemed to melt off him and disappear into a dark mist.

Naked the two figures grabbed around each other on the cold floor. Their lips locked and their tongues explored each other's mouths. Diego's tongue was cut against Dorian's fangs. Blood pulled into Diego's mouth, and Dorian began to drink it down as he slowly manoeuvred Diego onto his front.

The Soho Ripper

A gasp of pleasure escaped Diego's red lips as he felt Dorian fully enter him in a single thrust. Diego felt himself push back onto Dorian, forcing his obsession deeper and deeper. Strong hands grabbed Diego's hips, and he felt himself being lifted up. He faced the painting and saw the demonic figure grinning down at him as Dorian made love to him.

Cold sweat formed across Diego's body and his heart raced as his body tried to make sense of everything that was happening to him. Reaching back, Diego ran his fingers through Dorian's hair. Dorian then bit into the back of Diego's neck and kissed the wound as he thrust harder and harder.

Letting out a scream of pleasure and pain, Diego felt Dorian spill into him. For an instant which seemed to last an eternity, the two were one and the same. Their bodies had been fully joined, and each soul was able to explore where the atoms connected them. Flashes of memories, dreams, hopes and fears spilt out from one to the other.

Slowly and gently, Dorian pulled himself away from Diego and broke the connection. Then turning Diego's head, Dorian bit his own tongue and kissed Diego to pour more of his blood into him.

Then Dorian stood and walked over to the window. Outside it was raining, and the lights of London seemed to dance on the raindrops. Completely naked, Dorian looked out at the world, his face in a silhouetted profile and his firm butt pale in the dim light.

'Now, I must leave you, my dear.' Dorian cooed. 'You are on your own from now on, though I will check in from time to time. One word of advice, I'd be out of the way of these windows before the sun rises.'

Before Diego's eyes, Dorian picked up the painting and then his whole body and the portrait in his hands began to dissolve into a fine black mist. He whirled around and then disappeared into the shadow's leaving Diego alone as something primal and hungry formed within him.

The End.

The Soho Ripper

And now an extract from Book Two of the
Chronicles of Gaia,
Adrian Prince and the Crown of Shadows.

Prologue.
Transylvania, 1503.

The thick and bitter smell of smoke filled the damp
morning air in the dawn gloom. Mixing with the
sickly-sweet decay of rotting corpses, the stench
hanging over the mountain valley was repressive.

Standing on the edge of a cliff and looking down
at the mountain pass, Cesare Borgia looked down at
the battalion of slain men. The Ottoman army had
recently tried to march up the steep and narrow
mountain path to lay siege to Bran Castle. They
had, however, one and all been slain on the slopes
of the mountain and their bodies left to rot in the
summer sun of Wallachia.

A week later the army of the Cult of Rome had
arrived. Led by Captain General Cesare Borgia, son
of the Eternal Prophet Rodrigo Borgia. The Sacred
Armies mission was to rid Wallachia of its dark
ruler and bring it back into the arms of the Cult.
They had known about the advancing Ottoman
army, and Cesare was glad to see they had failed.

'Their failure will make our victory all the more
impressive.' The Captain General said to himself.

Joseph Willoughby-Rainsford

Clad in his full plate armour with a cloak of scarlet draped over his shoulders, Cesare struck a remarkable figure against the glare of the rising sun. Like all the officers in the Cult's army, Cesare's armour was coated in platinum and encrusted with amethyst. The properties of the precious metal and violet quartz were famous for being anti-magic. They were widely used by the warriors who fought against the sinister sorcerers and evil enchantresses.

'My Lord,' said one of Cesare's officers as he approached the stern-faced commander, 'the cannons are in position.'

'Then commence bombardment and prepare the army to move. I trust the artefact is ready?' Cesare said without peering back.

'Of course, my Lord.'

'Then I shall be the first to travel through it.'

The Captain General glanced up once more and took one more look at the castle. It was, in fact, three castles. The first and nearest was a walled courtyard around a massive central keep. It stood on the peak of a mountain ridge and so was only accessible by the steep, corpse covered pass. The rear two castles were both larger and taller than the one before. A bridge connected each of the castles.

Knowing well how dangerous mountain passes were for an army, the Eternal Prophet had not sent out his forces or his favourite son ill prepared.

The Soho Ripper

Within the vaults beneath the Cult's Grand Temple in Rome were many artefacts from the ancient Roman Empire. Objects forged by the Old Gods for the use of mankind. These and these alone were the only magical items allowed to be utilised by the agents of the Cult. Now one such item was in the possession of Cesare Borgia, and it would be the key to his victory.

'Cesare.' Said the excited voice of Alessandro Farnese.

A head shorter than Cesare, Farnese was young and bright-eyed with the look of wonder on his smooth face. He wore the plain robes of a Cultist Engineer. One of the few people trusted to study and work with the artefact, Farnese and his fellows were of vital importance to the Cult.

'Alessandro.' Cesare smiled with genuine affection to see his old friend.

The two young men had studied together at the Cult's most prestigious school in Piazza. There they had, quickly become friends, and in return to many helping hands in his education, Cesare had ensured Alessandro a prominent position in the Engineers.

'Isn't she a marvel?' Alessandro said pointing to the large device behind him.

To Cesare, the strange object appeared to be a massive ring of stone standing on end. Like the wheel of a giant's cart. At first, Cesare assumed there was a base to the stone ring, but on closer inspection, he realised it was floating.

'How old is that thing?' Cesare asked with a slightly worried glance at the cracks in the stone.

'That thing is called the Arcam Porta, and it's about a thousand years old, but she still works as well as the day Vulcan first forged her.' Alessandro said excitedly.

'And how exactly does that thing work?'

'Well…to be honest, nobody knows.'

'What?' Cesare looked at the stone circle and then back up to the magnificent castle on the peaks above.

'I assure you it is very safe. We had tested it before we left. It sent a large group of men across Rome in a matter of seconds.'

'Wasn't that the group of labourers who ended up in the Tiber?'

'Well, we have worked out what we did wrong since then. The following tests worked perfectly, and to be fair the device moved the men without trouble, it was just aimed poorly.'

'Who aimed it?'

Alessandro looked a bit shifty, '…I don't recall.'

Cesare rolled his eyes, but at that moment the cannons started to thunder. Along the cliffside where the cannons had all been set up, bursts of smoke rose. The cannons had fired in near perfect unison. They had been purchased from the King of

The Soho Ripper

Frankia. Their highly efficient and well-disciplined gun crews had come with them.

Before the rumbling had stopped echoing, Cesare's elite force, the Ducal Guard, bowed before their leader. Also, French, these highly trained and violent men were the younger sons of southern Frankia nobles. Each of them was a master of their weapon of choice, from swords and spears to axes and crossbows. There were no men on Gaia, Cesare trusted more to watch his back.

'The Ducal Guard and I shall be the first wave into the main courtyard of the castle. Then you shall send in the army, battalion by battalion at the assigned locations.' Cesare ordered Alessandro and the gathered officers. Then he walked up to a large wooden platform and looked down at his whole army spread out across the slope. Speaking out in a voice which echoed across the mountain side Cesare filled his men with hope and courage. 'This day we rid the world of a dark scourge. This being has been a plague upon these lands for too long and has driven the poor people of this region away from the loving arms of the Cult of Rome. In the name of the Eternal Prophet, and in the name of the Ancient Gods of Rome, we shall purge and purify this land.'

As a cheer erupted from his men, Cesare turned to face the hovering stone circle and his Ducal Guard. Giving Alessandro the slightest nod, Cesare then watched as his friend pulled out a small golden rod with a crystal in its end. The Captain General knew the device at once to be a Cult Activation Key, a device designed to spark approved arcane objects to life, without forcing the wielder to use magic themselves.

There was a flash of light and then a thunderbolt of blue energy flew from the rod into the centre of the floating ring of the Arcam Porta. As soon as the energy entered the upright circle, it stopped and oscillated around. Then the energy seemed to spiral outward and into the stone until it was completely absorbed. There were a few moments of silence and then nothing appeared to happen. About to say something, Cesare was shocked when before his eyes the fabric of reality ripped open in a flash of blue light.

'I told you!' Alessandro shouted over the sudden roar of wind being pulled into the portal. 'Now go! Quick!'

'Right men! Charge!' Cesare ordered after crunching a small paper pouch open into his mouth and feeling strength and energy flow through him almost at once, dashing forward before his men. They quickly followed in his wake but allowed their leader to be the first to enter the portal.

In the moments before he walked into the portal, Cesare closed his eyes. As soon as he entered the portal, he wanted to scream out but found there was no air in his lungs. It felt as if his body had been shredded into the smallest fragments. Each part was tossed around in a hurricane of energy.

Then without warning, Cesare stood in a courtyard before a stunned soldier. With a movement, too fast for the astonished soldier to block, Cesare drew his sword and sliced down cutting the man in two. As his bloody sword struck the snow, it reflected the beams of indigo flashes as the Ducal Guard appeared one by one in the courtyard around their leader.

'Take no prisoners!' Cesare shouted.

Before the poorly trained and poorly armed enthralled soldiers of the castle could form a proper defence, they were hacked down by Cesare's men. By the time the courtyard was covered with black and red uniformed corpses, cobalt flashes were appearing across the castle battlements.

The Captain General had to hold back his mirth. They had broken into the castle with complete ease and not lost a single man. Cesare knew; however, the brightly uniformed guards of Prince Vladimir were just for show and not the real strength of his so far unbeaten might. This castle was a large part of that strength, but the deadly enemies remained inside.

There was a blast of cannon fire, and Cesare saw the gunpowder filled cannon balls fly overhead and hit the rear towers of the castle. They exploded on impact in a shower of broken stone and smoke.

Seeing one of the towers collapse and disappear down the side of the mountain in a clatter of falling stones, filled Cesare with confidence. Victory was already at hand and would be his.

'Into the stronghold!' Cesare ordered. 'We take the throne room!'

The Ducal Guard rushed into the open gates of the castle's first keep. The great wooden doors were carved with the faces and heads of many wicked and horrific demons and beasts. As soon as they passed the doors, there was a flash behind them. Cesare turned just in time to see a large group of his men appear in the corridor before the wooden doors clanged shut.

The large hall within was dark and only lit by a few separated flickering torches, which hung too high up to be taken from their iron fixtures. From what little light there was, Cesare could see the musky red carpet on the floor and the grisly trophies on the walls. Prince Vladimir was infamous across Europe. His dark reputation had begun with the way he dealt with his prisoners of war.

Sticking out from the walls of the corridor every few meters were iron spikes, and on each one was the corpse of an Ottoman soldier. Even Cesare, who was no stranger to bloodshed, violence and carnage, felt his stomach turn at the ghastly sight. The Ducal Guard around him started to gag and mutter to themselves. Cesare could sense their resolve shaking.

'We move on unless you want to end up like them!' He snapped.

As a group, they rushed down the dark corridor. There was a loud rumble from overhead and dust, and stone fragments fell from the ceiling. The cannons were blasting apart the castle quicker then Cesare had expected. He had thought the stones of the castle would have been bound together with magic, like the fortresses of powerful mages, but perhaps he was wrong.

Reaching the end of the corridor, Cesare entered a large chamber filled with light and open to the elements. What had previously been the main audience chamber had half collapsed following the violent bombardment from the Cult's cannons. There was a door arch still standing, and from there a bridge extended across a great drop between the two mountain peaks. As Cesare watched, he saw the rear most structures of the Castle collapse down the mountain side as the cannon fire cracked the stone peaks. The sight was awesome to behold as tonnes of mortar and stone tumbled into a dark abyss.

The Captain General wondered how many of the vile creatures they had come to slaughter would have died trapped inside the crumbling walls. It was almost as if victory was upon them.

'Perhaps we didn't need to come up here,' One of his Ducal Guard joked, 'we could have sat back and watched the Gunners do all the work.'

There was a sudden slashing sound and then a thud. Cesare turned to find the Guard who had spoken standing without a head. Blood spurted from his neck like a small fountain as the helmeted head rolled to Cesare's feet. As the Guard's body fell to the floor, Cesare and the rest of his men saw the figure of a slight woman standing behind their fallen comrade.

She was dressed only in a light white night dress, which left nothing of her perfect form to the imagination. Her hair was jet black as were her eyes. She bore a wicked smile as she toyed with a ruby necklace, which rested in-between her round breasts. In her other hand, she held no weapon, but her whole arm was coated with blood.

'How will he watch without a head.' She giggled.

At once the Ducal Guard, who had seemed paralysed up until that point, aimed their weapons at her. The nearest two lunged for the woman, but she disappeared into shadow as her laughter echoed throughout the shattered hall.

The Ducal Guard surrounded their leader in a protective perimeter, looking into the shadows and holding their weapons at the ready. Cesare could hear his own heart rate racing in his ears. He had heard how fast the creatures could be, but he had never imagined it be beyond what human eyes could see.

There was a sudden scream. One of the Guards tried to swing his sword but was ripped apart by a shadow, which appeared to be only a blur of blood and gore. The next Guard to be attacked seemed to put up more of a fight, grabbing at something as his sword shattered in the iron grip of the woman. The Guard had managed to catch the female creature by the dress and necklace. The monster roared in his face, showing its terrible fangs.

Without hesitation, Cesare pulled a small bomb from his pouch and threw it at the creature. Upon impact the bomb exploded into a gust of thickly scented glittering smoke, leaving a falling cloud of twinkling silver shards and a rancid odour of garlic. The creature screamed in pain and ripped itself free from the necklace and dress.

It fell to the floor and scurried away on all fours like a strange crab or spider creature. As it left the cloud, Cesare saw something of the beast's true form. It had extremely long fingers, which ended in pointed razor claws. Its skin was sickly pale but lined with dark red veins which pulsed like fresh burn marks. The creature was also no longer beautiful but instead haggard with hollow cheeks, sunken eyes and bat-like features.

'Catina!' screamed the voice of another woman.

Joseph Willoughby-Rainsford

Looking up, Cesare saw a woman in a black dress flying over the bridge towards them.

'Aurora!' screamed the creature on the floor.

'So, you are Catina!' Cesare shouted, stepping forward to the beast, which was now almost on the edge of the castle ruins. 'You are one of the brides of Vlad the Impaler, are you not?'

'My master will suck you dry and gnaw on your bones, little tin soldier.' The creature on the floor hissed.

Cesare slowly walked forward as the creature tried to get away from him. Reaching the edge, the creature stopped and looked at him with real fear in its inhuman eyes. With a glance at the sky and the fast approaching new enemy, Cesare quickly pulled a bottle from his pocket and uncorked it. He grabbed the face of the creature and quickly shoved the phial into the creature's mouth as her jaws tried to snap on his fingers.

At once the creature screamed in pain as the silver solution burst out and flowed down her throat. Letting out a howl as her body began to catch fire from the inside, the creature tried to rip open its own throat to get the silver out. With hardly a glance, Cesare kicked the creature off the side of the broken castle and into the pit of bones and broken stone.

'Catina!' Yelled the second creature as it dived to catch her sister.

The Soho Ripper

The Ducal Guard lifted their crossbows and fired, but it was too late. The silver tipped bolts flew off and disappeared along with the two brides of Vladimir.

'We cross the bridge to the second Castle,' Cesare ordered, 'fire the flare.'

As one the Ducal Guard ran across the bridge as a green flare lit the sky over them. A few moments later the sound of cannon fire silenced.

Cesare and his men had to slowly and carefully cross the stone bridge between the first and second castles. It was cracked in many places, and in some sections, it was open to the abyss below it.

To make matters worse, a mist had gathered around them, making it impossible to see a few feet ahead. Close together the Ducal Guard moved across the bridge, watching for danger as their leader peered at the central Castle. Cesare thought he saw the flicker of movement from a red curtain and wondered if the infamous Prince of Shadows gazed unseen at his would-be slayer.

They were almost completely across the bridge when the front most guard lifted his hand to stop the group in caution. Cesare wondered if there was another break in the bridge when he heard what had stopped the Guard. It was the sound of a woman crying. The sound was horrible and pulled on Cesare's heart strings.

Joseph Willoughby-Rainsford

To him, it was the sound of his mother's weeping
when his brother had been found in the river Tiber
like a drowned rat, or the sound of his sweet
beloved sister's tears upon the death of her second
husband. The sound echoed in Cesare's mind and
brought up terrible memories he thought he'd left
behind.

'Move on!' Cesare ordered through gritted teeth.

Slowly they all crept forward until the mist
seemed to clear enough to show the open gates to
the second castle. Before them though was the
figure of a slender black haired woman weeping
over a broken corpse. The sound of the weeping
seemed to cloud Cesare's mind. He knew it was no
ordinary woman and yet he could only see his
mother or his sister weeping over the corpses of
their loved ones. The blurry image changed each
time he blinked, but Cesare forced himself to see
through the illusion and saw instead Aurora
cuddling the corpse of Catina.

'You did this!' the creature screeched at him.

The cry echoed in a bubble of pressure which
shattered the mist and caused the bridge to shake.
Then the creature leapt forward. Cesare and his
fastest men fell on their fronts. Those who did not
move in time where turned to ribbons of bloody
mincemeat across the bridge. Screams of pain and
suffering echoed out as men felt their bodies ripped

apart by a creature too fast to be seen by the human eye.

Cesare was about to force himself up as he felt a hand grab the back of his head. The creature lifted him up and threw him across the bridge and through the open doors of the second castle. Hitting the cold stone with a clatter, Cesare peered back to see the rest of his men being slaughtered like lambs unable to put on a fight against the fury and blood lust of the creature.

Then Cesare saw one of his men rise. He only had one arm, and his leg was clearly broken, and yet, somehow, he was able to find the strength to stand. The Guard pulled a bomb from his belt and closed his fist around it. As Cesare watched, the Guard punched his remaining fist directly at the face of Aurora. The beast opened her jaws wide and bit off the hand of the Guard, steel armour and all. The Guard fell backwards. A second later the creature exploded in fire and destruction.

By the time, Cesare was fully able to get to his feet, the smoke had cleared. The middle section of the bridge, the beast and all his men were gone. He was alone in the castle. With determination and before panic could set in, Cesare pulled a pouch from his pocket and sprinkled the contents on his tongue. At once, he felt his pain fade away, his mind become calm, and his strength return as the substance hissed within his mouth.

Closing his eyes and breathing deeply a few times, so the substance had time to enter his bloodstream and flow through his whole body, Cesare entered into a state of focus and inner strength.

'Thank you, father.' He whispered to himself, thinking how many times the substance known as Roman Nectar had given him the edge in battle.

Roman Nectar was another of the ancient inventions the Romans had created from magic to serve the common man. In truth, it was pure magic harvested from the blood of captured sorcerers, then dried and purified into fine powdered.

When a non-magical human ate the substance, as Cesare had many times before, their body went through a slight temporary change. It heightened all the person's sensors, increased their agility, speed and strength, and gave their mind the edge to be able to break through illusions. Cesare had snorted the substance on the night he had murdered his brother Juan, and dumped the body in the river Tiber. He had also rubbed the substance into his gums on the evening he had broken the neck of his sister's second husband as she had slept next to him.

As the substance flowed through him, though, those dark memories were pushed back to where they belonged. For good measure, Cesare poured more onto his tongue and as he did the carnage behind him faded away.

The Soho Ripper

The castle was dark and empty.

As Cesare searched from empty room to empty room, he thought the castle appeared to be more of a ruin than a residential palace of the Prince of a nation. Some rooms had lighter squares on the stonewalls, showing where pictures had once hung. Others were filled with broken and rotting furniture. In some rooms were piles of rusting armour.

Cesare found himself climbing stairs, going ever higher and higher in his search for Prince Vlad. At certain points, Cesare thought he heard echoing laughter. The Captain General also felt as if there was a presence watching him, but no matter how quickly he turned his head he never saw anyone.

'Come out you coward, and challenge me!' Cesare shouted.

His voice carried and echoed through the many empty rooms of the castle. Then a door to his left opened and let out a dull light. Entering the chamber, Cesare found a room within the castle furnished with finery. In the centre of the room was a four-poster bed with red sheets and curtains. Below the large arched window was a dressing table with a great mirror, framed with an elegantly curved pattern of hearts and bats.

Although the mirror only reflected the empty room, before it sat a woman on a stool. She was very slender and tall. Her elegant figure was contained in a black leather corset, while a dress of black leather ribbons flowed around her legs. The woman stared intently into the mirror, despite being unable to see her own reflection. Across her bear arms, Cesare saw many tribal tattoos done in black ink.

'I've been watching you,' the woman said in an exotic accent, unfamiliar to Cesare, 'you are looking for my husband.'

'Are you the third wife then?' Cesare asked, lifting his sword defensively.

The woman turned on her stall, so Cesare was able to see her startling beauty. Her hair was long and sleek, almost all black apart from a stripe of white hair in her fringe. Sitting completely still, this woman had far more of a regal and imposing pose then the other beasts Cesare had come across. Her eyes seemed to see through Cesare into his soul, and her slight smirk made Cesare believe she was amused by what she saw.

'Third wife.' She sighed. 'I am Livia, his second wife in truth, but the first woman he gave his dark gift too. That was so long ago. He was different then.' Livia glanced Cesare up and down. 'He was…like you. He knows you are coming for him. He waits for you upon the roof, but you won't kill him. Not with that.'

Livia gazed at the sword in Cesare's hand. Then she reached behind herself and lifted a small corked phial. Cesare tensed and made himself ready to strike.

'This is no threat to you,' Livia said, slowly getting up holding out the bottle to Cesare, 'it is a gift. Drink it, and you shall be able to harm my husband. The rest is up to you.'

'What is it?' Cesare asked, cautiously taking the bottle and glancing at the thick red contents.

'It is a few drops of my husband's blood, from back when he was only a human.'

'How will that help?'

'Dead blood is poisonous to us, and his own dead blood...doubly so.'

'Why are you helping me?'

For a short time, Livia did not answer as she walked slowly to the window and gazed out at the ongoing siege.

'In truth,' she said in a wistful voice, 'I'm only bored.'

'After I kill him, where will you go?'

'Somewhere you'll never find me.' Livia placed a hand on the window. The glass began to frost with ice.

'I'll come back for you one day. You realise that?'

Livia slowly turned and gave Cesare the same twisted smile. 'I look forward to it.'

It felt strange to Cesare to leave the vampire undisturbed in her boudoir. He turned towards the door and then felt a cool breeze against his neck. He looked back, and she was gone. All that was left was the curtain blowing gently before the open window.

Leaving the chamber behind, Cesare headed straight up the stairs without even glancing back.

He was completely focused on his task. In his right hand, he held his long silver sword, and in his left, he held the small phial. The phial was strangely cold to the touch as if it had been frozen. Cesare was torn on whether or not to use it. There was a good chance the phial was poison, but if Livia wanted him dead, then why did she not just kill him. He was not so arrogant to believe she couldn't have taken his life easily, despite the substance blazing through his veins.

'If it gives me a chance against Vlad, then I have little choice.' He reasoned with himself.

Normally under these circumstances, Cesare would have thought of Lucrezia, his beloved sister, but under the influence of the substance, his mind was unable to focus on anything but the task at hand. His emotions, fear and concerns were gone from his mind, and so he knew clearly what it was he needed to do and why.

Knowing with all certainty, it was the right thing to do, Cesare pulled out the cork from the phial with his teeth. He then drained the contents in a few gulps. The taste was similar to salt on his tongue, and at first, Cesare felt the need to gag as if he'd eaten something rotten. Then he coughed a few times and the taste seemed to fade away. Waiting a few seconds, Cesare was happily surprised when nothing happened.

He continued his climb up the tower steps, feeling a warmth of hope spread through his body.

The roof of the tower was open and flat. There were no walls to prevent someone walking off the edge. The only entrance was an open hatch which led to the spiralling staircase below.

Climbing out onto the tower, Cesare found himself completely exposed to the thrashing wind. From here he could see for miles. He saw the ruins of the rear most castle, the battle raging in the front most and the rest of his army on the slopes of the surrounding mountains.

There was one figure upon the tower top, who took all of Cesare's attention. He was tall and slender. Dressed in a fine frock coat over red and black steel, the figure was impressive and refined. His long black hair was held in a ponytail, tied back with ruby encrusted leather straps. On the top of his head, the beast wore a crown of gold with glowing firestones encrusted into the polished circlet.

The Captain General held up his sword defensively as he watched the creature before him.

The figure was staring at the battle raging within the walls of his own castle and seem to show no concern at all.

'You are Vlad the Impaler?' Cesare asked aloud.

'I am...Prince Vladimir Dracula.'

Cesare had blinked, and in that instant, the Prince of Darkness had moved from before him to behind him. Vlad walked calmly, his fingers interlocked as he observed Cesare through the corner of his eye.

'Are you the one they call the Duke Valentino?' the vampire asked in thickly accented Latin.

'I am Cesare Borgia. Captain General of the Divine Army, Defender of the Eternal Prophet and Marshal of the City of Rome.'

'So many beautiful titles.' Now Vlad was before Cesare again, walking along the very edge of the tower.

'I know a few for you. Prince of Wallachia. The Count. Prince of Darkness. The King…'

'Of Shadows.' Vlad was directly before Cesare, staring him right in the eye. They were less than an inch apart for only a second before Vlad returned in a blink to the edge of the tower. 'That title is my favourite, I must admit.' There was a note of humour in the vampire's voice. 'And I guess it is true.'

Vlad the Impaler stretched out a hand towards Cesare, and suddenly the Captain General found himself flying towards the Vampire. Dropping his sword in the shock, Cesare felt the long pale fingers of Vlad wrap around his neck as the Vampire held him over the edge of the castle with seemingly no effort.

Cesare clawed at the vampire's hand as he felt one of his boots fall off and disappear into the darkness below. Despite the substance flowing through his system he began to feel genuine fear grip him. Then his eyes were distracted by a growing shadow around Vlad. It was as if his dark aura was growing and coming to life.

'Now witness the power of the Crown of Shadows!' Vlad said, his laughter carrying on the wind.

The darkness around Vlad grew and began to take shape. Before Cesare's eyes, large demonic bats formed out of the black mist and swarmed all around the tower. The firestones in the crown upon Vlad's head glowed brighter as more demons began to appear. Then Vlad lifted his free hand and pointed. At once the swarm burst forth with thousands more demonic shadows flying from the abyss beneath the castle. So many flew into the skies above the mountain they blocked out the sun.

Turning his neck as much as he could, Cesare watched the swarm head towards his camp and the Arcam Porta. He watched as the swarm surrounded the portal and then compressed around it until nothing of the distant stone ring could be seen. Then the Arcam Porta exploded in a flash of bright blue light, destroying that part of the camp and the small section of the swarm. The rest of the outer reaches of the swarm then flew around the cannons, causing the men to flee in panic as each gun was ripped apart.

'See, this has only been a game.' Vlad said, his eyes glowing as red as the firestones above his brow.

Then to Cesare's amazement, the swarm began to lift the fallen pieces of the castle and place them back stone by stone as if the keep had never been destroyed. Within a matter of minutes, the castle was almost entirely restored. Then Vlad pointed to the rest of Cesare's army still on the mountain side and within the Castle.

Leaving his swarm to deal with the remainder of the invader's Vlad turned his now hungry eyes onto Cesare and his exposed neck. 'Your hot Spanish blood shall warm my cold heart as I watch my children feast upon your men.'

Then the Prince of Darkness opened his mouth impossibly wide and in a sudden movement sunk his fangs into Cesare. The Captain General felt a sharp pain as the pointed teeth tore into his neck. At once he felt the vampire venom begin to burn its way through his veins. At the same time, there was a sucking sensation as Vlad drank the blood gushing from Cesare's neck.

The Soho Ripper

Knowing he was not long for this world, Cesare reached for his dagger but then was shocked as Vlad pulled away from him, stumbled backwards and dropped him on the edge of the castle. Quickly pulling himself to his feet, Cesare held his dagger with one hand and held his neck with the other. He looked back at Vlad and saw the Vampire holding onto his chest in agony.

'Livia!' Vlad screamed. 'Livia! What have you done?'

Cesare's vision was beginning to go dark, but all around him, the swarm was still heading towards his army. Knowing this was his only chance, Cesare charged forward and plunged his silver dagger directly into Vlad the Impaler's chest. The Vampire looked up into Cesare's eye as the silver pierced his armour, broke his ribs and ripped into his cold dead heart.

The Captain General suddenly felt pain as the claws of Vlad cut into his chest and wrapped around Cesare's own heart. Cesare felt the creature tighten its grip. Blood burst forth from Cesare's mouth and onto the face of the vampire. As soon as the blood touched Vlad, his skin began to burn and then started rapidly melting away before Cesare's eyes.

Letting go of the dagger, Cesare reached up and pulled the crown from Vlad's head. At once the swarm disappeared as if it had never been. Then Vlad roared in pain until his body shrivelled up and collapsed into a pile of grey ash. With the crown in his hand's Cesare fell backwards. His head hit the hard stone as blood flowed all around him. In the distance, he heard the castle collapsing.

Knowing his eyes were still open, Cesare was shocked at how dark the world had become.

To be continued in Adrian Prince and the Crown of Shadows…

17573607R00081

Printed in Poland
by Amazon Fulfillment
Poland Sp. z o.o., Wrocław